3·2·77·

Antonia Parsons
from Sue, 2015

ETHEL MANNIN

Sunset Over Dartmoor

PHOTOGRAPHS BY F. W. ZIEMSEN

HUTCHINSON OF LONDON

are they known for typos?

Hutchinson & Co (Publishers) Ltd
3 Fitzroy Square, London W1

London Melbourne Sydney Auckland
Wellington Johannesburg and agencies
throughout the world

First published 1977
© Ethel Mannin 1977

Set in Monotype Baskerville

Printed in Great Britain by The Anchor Press Ltd
and bound by Wm Brendon & Son Ltd
both of Tiptree, Essex

ISBN 0 09 128010 9

For
my daughter, Jean,
without whom there would have
been no Overhill –
with love and gratitude

Acknowledgements

For the loan of works of reference I am gratefully indebted to Donald Hope, F.L.A., Borough Librarian, London Borough of Merton; for showing me much of Dartmoor and its villages, to my sister and her husband, Marjorie and Aubrey Saville; and for assistance with proofs, and the use of his photographs, to my old friend 'Tim' Ziemsen.

E.M.

Contents

Illustrations

PART I
Farewell to Oak Cottage

I

Oak Cottage, 1929-1974

In my observation and experience major events in personal life are not necessarily matters of decision; there comes a tide and you take it at the flood because it seems natural, somehow inevitable, that you should do so. Thus you do not necessarily 'decide' to get married – it just 'works out' that you should and do; you do not necessarily decide to change your job, but you have been fed-up for some time and somehow events have shaped to a change; you do not necessarily decide to have a child – but Nature has other plans; you do not necessarily decide to move house or to end a relationship, but places like relationships have a way of coming to an end, and it works out that you do; with no direct decision on your part it happens – is somehow decided for you.

Thus, when I returned to my Connemara cottage in 1963, after a year's absence, I did not know that I was doing so for the last time; I did not know until I got back to London that I would never be there again; but I knew, then, that it had come to an end. I did not have to make any decision.

The coming to an end of Oak Cottage was more protracted. During my long love-affair with Ireland – which went on for about twenty-five years – I at various times had fantasies of acquiring a house on Dublin's lovely Killiney Bay; and on and off I had fantasies of a house on Southampton Water or the Isle of Wight, and even consulted house-agents, but not until 1970 did I begin to feel that Oak Cottage had come to an end, that I needed a smaller and warmer house, and a smaller and more manageable garden, and to be near my daughter now that I had achieved my three-score-and-ten.

At that time I was thinking of a house-of-character in Exeter, a city I know and like, and where my sister and her husband live, and which would have been within reach of my daughter; but the house agents produced only ugly – and too big – Edwardian houses, or houses on modern estates, and I did not see myself in either. I continued to read the estate agents' lists, and the West Country property advertisements in the *Sunday Times*, but the fantasy faded a little. Reading 'the props' on Sunday is anyhow a game in which I fancy a good many people not seriously minded to move indulge. It is a form of escapism. Imagination leaps ahead and transfers you to that house – 3 beds. 2 recep. matured garden – overlooking the River Dart or the Falmouth estuary. You wonder, even, if you won't go down and look at it; only of course you don't. Fantasy doesn't call for action.

My Exeter inquiries, however, were not pure fantasy; I could imagine myself living in Exeter if a suitable house could be found, and increasingly I could not cope with Oak Cottage, with its too big garden, and its collapsing fences and pergolas – which increasingly I could not afford to renew. Also, after over forty years of it I was quite neurotically bored with the suburban roads of that select residential area, Wimbledon Common.

Then in 1973 the tall lovely elm trees that had formed so valuable a screen against the suburban scene, and afforded an illusion of the country when you set foot in the garden, were afflicted by that nation-wide curse, Dutch elm disease, and had to be reduced to telegraph posts, most hideous to behold. I had two bouts of Operation Elms in the garden, as first one group of trees and then another became infected, and after the second massacre – for it was that – I felt that I no longer wanted to go on living at Oak Cottage – that its great charm, that illusion of being in the country, had largely been destroyed.

Strangely, trouble-with-trees – tall pine trees brought down by a storm and lying across the stone walls, and inability to get them moved – had precipitated the end of the Connemara cottage. At Oak Cottage, too, the noble, 400-year-old oak tree had had to be reduced from sixty feet to twenty because of decay at the base, and now stood a gaunt ugly old hulk throwing out monstrous fungi from its hollow interior. Long ago I had thought that if ever the old oak went it would be a sign for me to go too, but I had hung on. Now the elms had also gone, and in the last year my favourite blossom tree, a crab-apple tree under which it had been so pleasant to sit beside the lily pond, had incontinently died – in that spring in which I had already mentally gone from Oak Cottage.

In November 1970, I recorded in my journal – which I keep daily – that I had had a fantasy of having a house 'near the bee-hive house' in a lane not far from my daughter. It is a Devon lane I had always liked, as it is high, overlooking the Teign estuary, and whenever I visited my daughter and we walked along it it had always seemed to me quite the pleasantest part of the area. I could imagine myself living there, in one of those attractive houses or bungalows standing on high ground, with their fine view. Then early in March 1974 my daughter telephoned me that there was a bungalow for sale there that might suit me. I went down to see it, and knew immediately that I could live there.

When I came to Oak Cottage in the summer of 1929, when I was twenty-eight and opting for independence, it was the realization of a dream, as I have recounted elsewhere,* since it was the house I had wanted for years, and it was most astonishing that when I was seeking a house of my own it should be on the market. The attraction it had always had for me – and which it retained to the end – was that it was unique – 'different'. In its suburban setting it nevertheless was something apart, set far back from the road, and with its towering ancient oak tree and its tall elms and little wood somehow conveying the feeling of being a country cottage. It was designed and built by an architect for himself, and he brought imaginativeness and loving care to its creation. He bought an old barn at Tunbridge Wells and used the massive timbers for the dining-room and hall, and for a brick-pillared pergola leading up to a tiled-roofed summer-house. For the steeply sloping roof of the house he had tiles

* In *Confessions and Impressions*, 1930.

specially baked, and hand-made; the guttering round the house was lead, with a handwrought design, and there were fine lead drain-heads. I have an idea that the guttering and drain-heads, like the massive studded oak front door, came from the house whose barn he bought, and regret that I did not discuss this with him, but at the time, 'young in the twenties', I was more interested in the 'picturesqueness' of the massive beams.

The dining-room opened on to a loggia, with a flagged path above, and a grassy slope leading up to the belt of tall elms. On this slope there was a seasonal succession of snow-drops, crocus, daffodils, bluebells. It was very pleasant to sit on the loggia, feet on the steps up to the path above, with drinks, coffee, tea, and many sat there in the early thirties that were the overflow from the 'gay twenties' – Allen Lane, a handsome and amusing young man who had not then started Penguins and thereby launched himself on the road to a title and millionairedom, the witty author, Louis Marlow, the young and pretty Christina Foyle, already organizing her famous luncheons, the novelist, Douglas Goldring, Violet Hunt brooding on her memories of Ford Madox Hueffer, Ralph Straus, most amiable of *Sunday Times* literary critics, the celebrated photographer, Paul Tanqueray, who had photographed 'everyone', social, literary, theatrical; and many others. There were lunch parties, dinner parties – with red candles under the old oak beams – cocktail parties with dancing to the wind-up H.M.V. gramophone. 'Hadn't we the gaiety?'

The outbreak of World War II ended an era, and during and after the war the guests at Oak Cottage – with the exception of old friends – tended to be more political than literary. Though already before the war I had joined the Independent Labour Party – at the invitation of Fenner Brockway – and became more politically orientated. The local branch of the I.L.P. met every week at Oak Cottage; we sat round the long table in the oak-beamed dining-room and passed resolutions, planned meetings and propaganda campaigns, and generally plotted the Revolution. We gave what we called 'critical support' to the U.S.S.R., and addressed each other as 'comrade'. Comrade Mannin served drinks – beer and stout – to the other comrades on their arrival, and coffee at half-time. A Marxist member of another branch denounced us at a party conference as 'the most bourgeois branch in the Party'. The comrades were nothing if not doctrinaire. But certainly it was a very cosy branch.

(I met Reginald Reynolds, whom I was to marry in 1938, at an I.L.P. dance in 1935. We both eventually left the Party, Reginald in 1939 over the Palestine issue – which he had closely at heart – as he tells with some passion in his autobiography, *My Life and Crimes* (1956); I have forgotten in what year I resigned, but it had to do with my growing disillusion with the U.S.S.R. and along with it the feeling that I did not belong with the Party. After I resigned, Oak Cottage continued to be the meeting place of the local branch for some years.)

When the Spanish Civil War broke out in the mid-thirties Reginald and I, and other I.L.P.-ers, became interested in the Spanish anarchists in their revolutionary struggle against Fascism on the one hand and Communism on the other. The veteran Russian-American anarchist, Emma Goldman, came to London; Reginald and I became involved with her and worked with her and the London anarchists in support of the Spanish comrades. It thus eventuated that Emma became one of the overnight guests at Oak Cottage at some point. I gave her my room for the night and filled it with roses from the garden, but she moved them all out on to the landing when she went to bed, as though it were a hospital ward. She was not an easy guest. Knowing of her love for German wine I bought a bottle of vintage hock for dinner, and inquiring of her if the wine was to her liking received the disheartening reply, 'Well, dear, it isn't *cold* enough, and it isn't *dry* enough, but it will do!' Reginald soon wearied of her ungraciousness and aggressiveness as a person and her dictatorialness as a comrade, and could not, in any case, as a pacifist – he was a Quaker and had worked with Gandhi in India – support her arms-for-Spain campaign, but I, who was not then a pacifist, struggled along with her to the end, and Spanish anarchists used a room at Oak Cottage as an office. Later a group of London anarchists stole a printing press from the Communist H.Q., and duly delivered it at Oak Cottage; it was housed in the summer-house until Reginald and I decided that really we could not be the receivers of stolen goods, even though stolen from our hated enemies, and ordered its removal. After that our relations with the anarchists suffered a setback.

But angry black men came, discoursing vehemently about 'freedom for Africa', and Reginald and I supported something called the African Freedom Campaign, eminent in which was our West Indian friend, George Padmore, who was to become Kwame Nkrumah's right-hand man. Learie Constantine – who was to dream he would ever become a peer? – was there with his Trotskyist comrades who never stopped talking, so that all I had to do was to pour the tea and pass the sandwiches. The gracious and beautiful Mrs Pandit, then Indian High Commissioner in London, came to tea; W. B. Yeats came for the weekend. . . . Oak Cottage knew its celebrities, literary and political, but many who were not – nor destined to be – but simply dear friends who were free-lance journalists, painters, small-part actors, and people who just got along as best they could. Celebrities or nonentities, they talked and laughed in the sunshine over drinks on the loggia, or in the book-lined sitting-room over tea, or wined and dined under the oak beams, the laughter rising and the world put to rights, or taken apart.

Later in the day came the Arabs, passionate and bitter – that most violent of Christians, the Palestinian George Mansour – who once brought me some gladioli, having been told that when visiting an English lady you take flowers, and thrust them at me like a sword – and the Lebanese author, Edward Atiyah, and Dr Izzat Tannous, who with George Mansour founded the Arab Centre in London.

There was all that, but Oak Cottage also knew its love-affairs and was many times a haven for lovers. It knew all the joys of love, licit and illicit, and all the recriminations and scenes. A great deal of life was lived, one way and another, at old 'Oaky Cott', as it became affectionately known to those who enjoyed its hospitality. It had its intensely personal history – as all old houses have.

Of all this I was deeply aware when I decided to leave it. I knew that I was turning my back on the major part of my life. I had written so many books, done the bulk of my work, in the book-filled study overlooking the lily-pond, with the rose-garden terraced above it. But it had come to an end. By 1970 it had become all too much in the garden, too many rose-beds and borders to hoe, too much grass to cut, too many paths to weed; and the place needed an injection of money I could not provide. The fences were precariously propped up with posts, tied up with string, and I could not spend any more money on fencing – which is expensive; the two elm tree operations, and a third operation to inject the remaining trees against disease, ate up money. In the house the kitchen was hideously in need of redecoration, and all over the house the leaded windows needed attention – some could not be opened because they were off their hinges and if opened could not be closed again; others when closed would disport gaps inches wide. In despair I consulted a local Irish builder – couldn't he repair the windows? 'Ah no,' said he, ''twould be cheaper to have new windows entirely!' I suggested that perhaps I should have new windows. 'Ah no,' he said again, 'twould be too expensive altogether!' He manifestly did not want the job. I despairingly indicated two out of three windows in the room in which we stood and which I could not open. 'Sure,' said he, 'there are other windows ye can open!' At which point I gave up. I had tried, but it was no good. This Irish builder had been my last hope. There are times when life is against one. Nobody can be bothered with small fiddling jobs nowadays; It's not worth anyone's while; if you want your whole house repainted, costing hundreds of pounds, it's another matter . . . but it still won't get the small jobs done. I know. I've tried.

It just was all, increasingly, too much; I tired of the struggle, and increasingly scoured and scoured the house-agents' lists for a house in the West Country. There was, too, the consideration, and it was considerable, and increasingly demanding attention, that if I sold Oak Cottage and bought something for half what I got for it I would have a little capital, and a little capital brings a little income, and thus I might be able at least to semi-retire, writing only one book a year instead of two. After fifty years of professional authorship, and for many years past turning out two books a year, on average, I felt myself entitled to that. All in all, a move was indicated; it would give me a new lease of life on the last lap. If only I could find the right place.

Then in March 1974 my daughter rang with the news of the house for sale 'near the beehive house' of my 1970 fantasy, and after visiting it twice I put Oak Cottage on the market – after forty-five years.

2

Order to View

When I still believed that I would finish out my allotted span at Oak Cottage – that is to say, before 1970 – the Irish builder who didn't want to repair the windows had me promise him that if ever I decided to sell the place I would give him the first offer, and, said he, 'I'll give ye the highest market price for it!' He was charmed with the place; it was 'different', he said, and he called it his 'retirement cottage'. I took him so seriously that I even put it in writing for him that when I died my daughter would give him the first offer, and for this he warmly thanked me. Thus, when I knew that I wasn't after all going to 'finish it out' at Oak Cottage it was natural to ask him if he was still interested, and he assured me that he certainly was – and made the first of a series of visits with foot-rules measuring the rooms and the garden fences. I confidently assured the Devon house-agent with whom I was dealing over the bungalow that I had a buyer for my London house, and he said I was very lucky, for the 'market' was 'very difficult' just now. The only problem with my prospective purchaser was the price. What did I want for the place? I simply did not know; I only knew what houses in the area fetched – neo-Georgian villas for fifty-four thousand, and that sort of thing. I had no idea what sort of price Oak Cottage, which was unique, should command. I wanted the builder-man to make me an offer. When he consistently declined to do this, insisting that I must know what I wanted for the place, I put the matter in the hands of an estate agent.

The man from the estate agency was the first viewer. He was late-middle-aged, heavy, unforthcoming, and un-impressed. He did not do more than glance at the garden from the dining-room door. The place wanted a lot doing to it, he said, morosely; for one thing there was no central heating; there was also no garage, though, he acknowledged, plenty of room for one. We could let the place go to the interested party for 'something in the region of fifty-five', but if we 'went public' we could ask fifty-nine five hundred. I found these figures staggering, but indicated that I would sooner sell to the Irish builder for less, because I wanted him to have the place and had promised it to him – he had even, I confided, offered to buy it years ago with me in it, to finish my life out there, to make sure of it, but I hadn't liked the idea of finishing out my life in a place no longer my own. The man from the estate agency appeared unimpressed by the story. But he telephoned the Irish builder and told him what he could have it for, 'or near offer', and what we would ask if we 'went public'. The potential buyer was non-committal. He would have to look into his finances, he said, and would let me know next week. That I had a buyer for Oak Cottage no longer seemed so certain. But I was prepared to wait.

There were telephonings and comings-and-goings, and at the end of the month the Irishman called off at fifty thousand. He and his wife had decided that the place was too small (she had in fact not seen the inside of the house) and by the sale of their own house they'd only just 'get by'. He was really sorry, but there it was.

I was then in the position of having confidently contracted to buy the Devon bungalow – with no ready money with which to do so. Banks at that time were sticky about 'bridging loans', and mine referred me to the building society in which I had the entirely inadequate sum of two thousand pounds; the building society referred me to the bank. . . .

There are times when life is against one, as I have said, but there are also times when it comes up and begs one's pardon, and it did so this time. Two things happened: a life-long fan, hearing of my predicament, said she had just inherited a legacy of fourteen thousand pounds and it was sitting in her deposit account doing nothing and was at my disposal, interest-free. The other thing was that an elderly cousin, whom I had not seen since I was about sixteen, died and left me half of her savings, several thousand pounds. It meant that though I still hadn't the money to buy the Devon bungalow, I had half the purchase price – more than enough to secure it – and a mortgage was arranged for the rest. The interest on the mortgage was frightening, but I would surely sell Oak Cottage now that we had 'gone public', and I was all set to settle for fifty thousand for a quick sale. Never in my life had I had to think so much about *money!*

Then began the procession of viewers. Anyone who has ever sold his residence – as opposed to merely selling a house in the way of property dealing – will know with what mingled trepidation and eagerness one both looks forward to and shrinks from viewers. Showing strangers over one's home – with all its imperfections, which one's friends never notice, and which until then one had oneself always taken for granted and not thought much about. Hitherto one had always shown the house with pride – the old oak beams, the fact that from the sitting-room 'you can't see any houses', the illusion of the country from the loggia. Now one is acutely aware of all the defects – the lack of central heating, no garage, the rising damp in the outside W.C., the kitchen that so badly needs redecorating and is really a disgrace, the strip of paper peeling off over the stairs, the damp patch in the front bedroom. . . . As to the windows you just hope no one will notice; the thing is to open those that will open, thus concealing the gaps when they are closed.

The garden, anyhow, is beautiful – despite the elms reduced to telegraph posts and the dead crab-apple tree. The azaleas and bluebells are out, and there is wistaria on the wall of the house, and the fish swimming around in the pond. That is at the outset, in the spring, but the viewing goes on all through the summer, and by then there are the roses, and the lilies on the pond.

'Of course, it's really a rose garden,' I hear myself saying, over and over again – after I have said my piece about the oak beams in the dining-room coming from an old barn at

Tunbridge Wells. As time wears on I begin to feel with every viewer, like an official guide reeling off the regulation patter. Entering the dining-room, I always began, 'Of course, this was a house built by an architect for himself' . . . then on about the old barn and the beams, and on, outside, to the handwrought lead guttering and the handmade specially baked tiles for the roof; then the tour of the garden – with which they were always charmed. The two things certain to impress were the oak-beamed dining-room and the garden.

What was interesting about the viewers was that the young ones were more impressed than the middle-aged ones; it was the young ones who found the place romantic, and the middle-aged ones who murmured, 'Of course it all wants a lot doing to it.'

The first viewers were late middle-aged and very nice . . . but the house was too small for them and too much in need of 'modernization'. They had a pleasant house locally, but were threatened with 'development' near by. They invited me for a drink and to see their house, and I duly went, and thought how bright and light it was, and couldn't imagine them leaving it for dark old Oak Cottage.

More viewers came two days later, the man tall and dark and Semitic and uncommunicative, the woman yellow-haired and white-booted and friendly; the man didn't bother to tour the garden but stayed chatting with the estate agency man who accompanied them whilst I showed Mrs X round the garden, which she thought lovely, but I knew when they left that I had no hopes of them – and couldn't anyhow for the life of me imagine them living there.

The next viewers were young and they thought everything charming, but they needed two bathrooms, and a paddock for their pony.

Then there was a young-middle-aged couple, pleasant enough, but I recorded in my journal, 'but I don't think they are serious'.

A few days later, despairing, I had another estate agent come and assess the place. He talked of putting a 'realistic' price on the place, to which I readily agreed. But I wrote in my journal, 'I feel that no one wants poor old Oak Cottage now. It's not what people want; they want two bathrooms and central heating and double garage, and nothing like so large a garden. People don't want gardens, nowadays; they want patios. As a friend said, "in the past so many people must have said, 'if you ever sell Oak Cottage give me the first offer.'" and it's true, but where are they now? Dead, most probably!'

Easter intervened and there was a lull on the viewing front, then a couple came with a name that I wondered about – was it perhaps Italian? It could even be Arab. It proved to be Egyptian, and I was so delighted to meet an Egyptian again that I recklessly gave him my file copy of the out-of-print *Aspects of Egypt*. He and his wife liked the house and garden very much, with the rider that it wanted a lot doing to it, and I got the feeling that they wouldn't buy it. They nevertheless came a second time to view it, this time bringing their children. But they decided that they really wanted four bedrooms and a study, and Oak Cottage could only offer three and a study. They invited me to dinner and I agreed to go, but when the time came felt too nervously exhausted and called it off.

Then there was a tall bearded man, an architect, and his wife; they admired the garden, but what they felt about the house I have no idea.

I invoked the aid of Harrods, and a pleasant woman came and admired the house and garden and said perhaps the place would appeal 'to a young executive'. . . .

Then a Swede offered thirty-seven thousand cash for the house without seeing the inside!

Then a doctor and his wife, who thought the garden 'fantastic'. They rang back in the evening to ask if they could come again at the weekend with her mother. They were young-middle-aged; trendy.

Then another doctor, a pathologist, and his wife, and to them I very much wanted to sell the house, for they were my kind of people and I could imagine them and their children living there. They very much wanted the place, but the snag was that they had to sell their own house first . . . and if anyone who wanted to buy their house had to sell their own house first it could be an endless chain, I realized despairingly.

But I wanted so much to sell to them that I felt it had to happen.

But it didn't. The Swede came back with his girl-friend and this time saw the inside of the house and offered forty-five thousand cash, which he was able to do because he worked in a bank and the money could be made available. I had to decide by mid-day the next day. I felt I was being stampeded, and I wanted the pathologist and his family to have the place, and I did not see the Swede and his girl-friend living there. I decided to turn down the cash offer and wait for the family I wanted, and when I had decided this felt much better. It was, of course, crazy. I had allowed myself to be sentimental over the sale of the Irish cottage in the sixties and should have known better. We live but we do not learn, as Somerset Maugham wrily observed. Unable to sell their own house quickly the pathologist and his wife finally withdrew. The doctor and the mother-in-law came back with an offer of forty-one thousand, and I said it wasn't on. There was a couple with three children after that, and a Persian and his English wife, and an uncommunicative middle-aged American with an Australian young woman who might have been his girl-friend or his secretary. He was poker-faced and said nothing at all; she liked the garden; they came and they went, and I had no hopes of them.

I had, by then, by the end of May, no hopes at all. Meanwhile I had a mortgage on the Devon place at $13\frac{1}{2}\%$ for three months, and 16% after that. The man from the first estate agency declared that it was 'early days yet', but I felt that it had all been going on for years. It was actually only two months, but I was nervously exhausted – and desperately tired of thinking about money. I wrote in my journal, 'I am very, very weary of it all!'

In July there was a Jewish family, with children, whom I liked, and who were all set to make an offer for the house, but his finances didn't work out – which, since he was himself 'in property', was a surprise and a disappointment both to me and to the estate agents. I would have liked them to have the place.

The day this family came there came also a young man and his wife and little boy of three; the wife was expecting another child in a few days' time. They liked the house and were set to make a cash offer of forty thousand. I liked them and could imagine them living there, but was sceptic of his bank advancing the amount.

He came to see me a few days later and said, laughing, 'You thought I wouldn't get the money, didn't you? Well, I did!'

If his surveyor's report was satisfactory it was the end of the road.

The report wasn't satisfactory; the drains were gone. The deal went through, all the same.

After that there was a procession of architects and surveyors, with measurings-up and drawings to scale. The young man and his wife and I soon became on Christian name terms. He gave me an engraved glass whisky decanter, and I gave him all my books in print, he having said he wanted everything I'd ever written. . . .

It was the end of July, and hot and humid. There were last visits to Oak Cottage, and trips to Devon to see about redecorations and carpets, and arrangements made for the Big Move.

I had got there, but I was very tired. It had all used up all the spring and summer and now it was the first days of September.

3

The Big Move

People said, sympathetically, that moving after forty-five years would be a 'traumatic experience'; in fact it wasn't, for I had long gone from Oak Cottage in my mind and wanted only to be gone in the flesh. Also a good removal firm makes it all very easy, and my admiration for the efficiency of removal men is unbounded. Every removal job must necessarily be different, varying with the size of the premises and the amount of goods to be moved, and their nature. My own problem was books – some two thousand of them. The rest of the stuff amounted, really, to very little.

The removal firm made a three-day operation of it. On Day One they came in and packed the books – forty-six tea-chests of them, most of them in my study, so that I sat that night barricaded in by them, and beyond the barricade the gauntness of empty shelves and bookcases. The next day, Day Two of the operation, they removed the tea-chests and the rest of the stuff – and on that day I moved down to Devon to spend the night with my daughter. The following day, Day Three, the pantechnicon moved off to Devon, arriving mid-afternoon, and I moved in. There was even a Day Four, when a man from the local branch of the firm came to un-pack the books and remove the empty tea-chests to the garage.

On the actual move-in day the removal men are at the peak of their efficiency, whilst you gradually sink to a low level of mental, nervous, and physical exhaustion; they march about clutching improbably huge items – 'Where you want this, love?' – and you'd better know where all is to go. They reassemble the wardrobe, likewise the dressing-table, 'and we'll get your bed up for you, love,' to Love's relief – and all that worry you had about whether they'd ever get the big old settee in at the front door is so much expense of spirit in a waste of no-necessity, for two of them pick the monster up as though it were no more than a shopping bag and deposit it where you want it – and of course it goes through the front door, on its side, quite easily.

Physically the removal men make it all very easy for one, such is their efficiency, but also they are remorseless. No bit of clutter is left behind, down to the last brown paper bag you had omitted to throw out. Their instructions are to remove *everything*; and they are completely faithful both to the spirit and the letter of the law. Those battered old baking tins you'd thought you might leave behind in the drawer at the bottom of the cooker – they fish them out and they are duly unpacked from their newspaper wrapping in the new place. That half bottle of ink you thought you'd just leave on the study mantelpiece, that beastly bottle of salad cream you've had for years and will never use, bought by mistake, and which you'd thought you could just leave on a shelf in the larder for the new owner to use or throw out – ruthlessly all are wrapped in newspaper and packed. Your cheating, sloppy, slip-shod ideas haven't a chance against the experience and efficiency of the removal men. They've met your kind before many times. If you've a lot of junk you'd thought you might now jettison you should have thought of it earlier. Once the removal men are in they remove the lot – that is the contract.

You feel you ought to remember what was the first thing to be carried into your new home, but you don't – anyhow, I didn't. I only know that I had forty-six tea-chests of books parked in the entrance hall – fortunately large – and that packing cases of china and glass, and pots and pans, were unpacked in the kitchen and the items, excavated from endless newspaper wrappings, stowed away in new, un-familiar cupboards; that items of furniture were placed in position in rooms, and once the bed is up there is a feeling of security – you can at least go to bed! – and somehow, after a few non-stop hours of it, you are, astonishingly, approximately straight. At some point you make tea; I did, but have no recollection of doing so; all I remember is that eventually I had a tot of whisky and passed the bottle round to the men, asking the foreman if he'd like a drink, and he replying that he 'wouldn't say no'. Then we all leaned for a bit – all except the old friend who had come down from town to help with the move-in and who declined this refreshment and just doggedly carried on unwrapping and putting away. By midnight there remained only the forty-six tea-chests of books.

How people can move house often, as some do, I find baffling, for though the efficiency of the removal men makes it physically easy for one, it still remains a major operation – not necessarily a traumatic experience, but definitely an exhausting one, mentally and physically. There is the confusing aftermath, too, in which things can't be readily found – where is the hammer, and where did we put the tea-strainer?

Within a week, of course, all that is over, and it's as though you'd never been anywhere else. Though with me the books presented a problem. To get some two thousand books, fiction and non-fiction, poetry and plays, sorted and re-arranged into some semblance of an organized library, such as they had been before the move, was a nightmare, and by the end of a week of it, working all day and half the night, I came almost to hate books. Why had I accumulated so many? Did I really want them all? I had got rid of two or three hundred before I left London – why hadn't I got rid of more, whilst I had the chance? If they could have been emptied from their crates into heaps of biographies, political works, travel books, philosophical and religious works, novels – but in whatever order they had been removed from their London shelves when they were emptied out at their new destination they were an unsorted chaos of fiction and non-fiction. To come upon a pile of books about anarchism, and another pile about Buddhism, constituted a windfall of order in the chaotic wilderness; then suddenly the blessedness of a 'corner' in fiction, all the Irish novels in a heap . . . but then a confusing miscellany in which every volume has to be scrutinized and placed with the appropriate collection. Gradually, however, after days and nights of it, and a great mental weariness, the shelves filled up in some sort of order – the Middle East shelf, the Japan shelf, the Irish shelf; the bookcase of poetry and plays was restocked, the novels sorted into Irish, Russian, French, German, English, American; the books about ballet, the miscellaneous, not easily classifiable books, all were duly accommodated in reasonable order . . . though I can no longer go unerringly to a shelf and lay hands on any book. That is going to take some time yet – and it is months, as I write. Also every now and then I come across a book in the wrong place – Gerald Brenan's *Spanish Labyrinth* in amongst the travel books, even a non-fiction amongst the fiction – and I have, too, not been able to classify as strictly as I would wish, so that some of the biographies and autobiographies have had to overflow away from the main body of these works. This is grievous, but the shelf space is such that there is no help for it. Happy those, I suppose, for whom books are just books, to be shoved up on shelves and into bookcases any old how – 'irregardless'.

The Big Move wasn't the ordeal I had expected it to be, not when it came to it, but there were all the anxieties beforehand – minor, though they seemed major at the time; anxieties as to whether the redecorations would be completed at the new house, the carpets laid, the gas, electricity, telephone connected. . . . It does, of course, all get done before you move in, but it does all represent anxieties – problems, even. I was very fortunate in having my daughter at the other end to supervise the redecorations, hang curtains, attend to innumerable details, and in having her and a good friend to help with the move-in; without such devoted help it would all have been very much more exhausting, very much more difficult.

I was fortunate, too, on Day Two, the day of the move-out, to have a good friend in the form of a neighbour across the road to go to for a drink and a snack when I had turned the key in the massive front door of my old home for the last time. Without this very considerable – and considerate – amenity there would have been nothing for it but to trek off drearily alone to the railway station and the train for Paddington and the West Country. As it was I spent a pleasant hour or so, had no 'trauma' about the move-out, and was duly taken to the station by car and seen off.

I was, altogether, very fortunate throughout. I had my daughter to go to for the night before the move-in – and a champagne-supper welcome to the West Country. I had everything for which to be grateful, and I was and am. To move to a district where you know no one, and have no one to help you on arrival, takes courage, I think, though very many do it – but married couples, rather than solitaries such as myself.

In leaving London, where I was born and bred, and where I lived all my life except for interludes in Paris and Vienna, I was leaving a city that no longer had anything for me, with its traffic density, noise, pollution, pornography. In recent years I seldom went 'into town'. When I did it was only on missions to my publishers, which was usually a matter of straight there and back. I was leaving valued friends, but the Inter-city trains are fast, and I was only going three hours away.

But though the Big Move wasn't either physically or psychologically the ordeal I had anticipated, all the same I was glad it was a once-in-a-lifetime experience. The next move, across the river Styx, will be easier, if less interesting. Charon is the ultimate Removal Man.

Top Overhill, with author

Above Overhill, overlooking the River Teign to the Haldon Heights

Top Teignmouth, from Shaldon

Above Teignmouth: the docks, looking across to Shaldon

4
Settling-in

Moving to a village cannot be the anonymous affair moving to a town is; in a village a newcomer is an object of interest, and when the newcomer is a well-known writer the interest is naturally intensified. Thus, in the first few weeks in this Devonshire village I was constantly accosted on my morning expeditions to the shops by pleasant strangers who smiled and said Good-morning and added that they hoped I would be happy there. The vicar called and expressed the same wish; I am, of course, a dead loss to him, but he was not to know that – unless he had read my books – and it was anyhow his duty to call on the new parishioner. Later on the people who had first accosted me hoped that I was 'settling-in'. I assured them that I was . . . as I assured the friends who wrote from London.

Actually the settling-in process is swift and painless. Once you have your furniture arranged in approximately the same positions that it occupied in your old home, and have your books sorted out and settled on their new shelves, and have got used to the new kitchen arrangements, so that you no longer wonder where the tea-strainer is, you may be said to have settled in. Certain psychological readjustments have to be made, though, and this takes rather longer. After I had been here several months I found myself referring in conversation to some domestic habit I had 'at home' – by which I meant the home I had known for forty-five years, a clear indication that despite the external acceptance of the new environment the unconscious was still tied to the past, and had not, in fact, settled in. My daughter, who came here in 1945, found that for a long time she thought of herself as merely on holiday here, and caught herself out thinking what she would do when she 'got back.' Walking along a crowded seaside promenade or waterfront, thronged with holiday-makers, it is in fact difficult to realize that you are not one of them, or 'down for the day', but are a resident – though being a resident by no means makes you a native. The native Devonians in this village are rare; the majority of residents are immigrants like myself, people from all over, from London, the Midlands – many from the Midlands – the North, and even unlikely places like Ross-on-Wye. They have come here in retirement, perhaps, because they had holidays here and liked it and ear-marked it for retirement, or they have come in widowhood to be near a married son or daughter. The result is that this is a village full of middle-aged and elderly people; there are a few young people – young women pushing prams – but the majority are elderly. This I knew before I came here, and when I was relatively young myself I held it against the place. Of course, it was charming, I used to say, with its waterfront and boats and 19th century houses round the green, but such a very elderly *retired* place. . . . In later years the fact no longer applied as a criticism.

People ask me if I miss London, and the answer is an emphatic no, for even though I lived only nine miles from Charing Cross I seldom went into town in those last years, as I have said; asked if I miss Oak Cottage the answer is 'not really', which means 'in a sense'. I think of it with mixed feelings. The best years of my life were spent there, and a great part of the later years. It was beautiful, and it was unique, but in the later years there was the despairing feeling of being unable to cope; there were the collapsing fences, the mutilated trees, the dilapidation in the house itself, and my almost neurotic boredom with the suburban roads I had been traipsing for forty-five years to the shops of the so-called 'village'. Here I walk along the estuary to the shops, and either the tide is out, with long stretches of wet sand and seaweed, or it is in and brimming like a full bath, and then the swans come floating in, regally; when it is out there are the little turnstones turning the pebbles, and the lovely black

and white oyster-catchers, and the varieties of gulls assembled
on their feeding-grounds – and people poking about in the
wet sand for bait for fishing, and coloured boats keeled over
awaiting the tide to float them, and bobbing red and
yellow buoys out in the channel. And always in the distance
there is Dartmoor, clear and blue and mountain-ridge, or
half enveloped in massed cloud. Most mornings I walk
along the water, and people say Good-morning, women
with shopping bags and baskets, elderly men walking their
dogs, and I could never become bored with it as with the
suburban roads, because with nature the scene is always
changing, and always, in a strange way, come high-water or
low, dramatic. You cannot be bored by the ebb and flow of
tides, the wheeling of gulls, the bobbing of boats and buoys,
the massing of clouds on hills, the changing light and shade
on water. I had been familiar with all this before I had come
to live here, but once I had come to live it had become part
of my daily life – part of the settling-in. The pleasure in
the white sea-horses on the water on windy days, and in the
primroses on the banks of the high-hedged lanes in the
spring are all part of the settling-in process. In this identi-
fication there is content, and the old life recedes into
unreality. When that happens you have truly settled-in.

The house for which I abandoned 'old Oaky Cott' is a
modern split-level bungalow standing on rising ground
above a shallow valley that was once an orchard and is now
full of scattered houses and bungalows; at the far side
orchards rise steeply to a ridge. There are some fine mimosa
trees in the valley, and from the house, which is called
Overhill, there is a view out over the Teign estuary to the
Haldon heights. The house has this in common with Oak
Cottage – that it is 'different', having been, like Oak
Cottage, designed by a man for himself. It neither looks nor
feels like a bungalow, and is not a bungalow in the accepted
sense, for there are indoor stairs down to a workroom, out
of which the garage opens. When you come in at the front
gate the drive leads along between apple trees to the garage,
and a short slope leads up to the front door – and there is a
fine view out over the water. The garden is on different
levels – again like Oak Cottage – and there is a grassy hollow

with apple trees, the remains of the orchard site on which the house was built.

The garden had gone wild with weeds and long grass by the time I moved in, but remaking the garden is part of the process of settling-in, and once the grass has been cut, and the weed-grown beds and borders dug, comes the exciting business of planting – following the exciting business of long ponderings over nurserymen's catalogues. I wanted a rose-garden again, and I wanted all the old favourites I had successfully cultivated at Oak Cottage, and there was a hedged, sheltered square of garden ideal for a rose-garden. Some fifty rose-bushes went into it. I planted, also, azaleas and fuchsias, and some trees including eucalyptus, which thrives, like mimosa, in the West Country. I am fortunate in having, at one corner of the garden, near the rose-garden, a big old mimosa tree which becomes golden in January and goes on blooming down into March.

I have had the house of the weeping willow tree, about which I wrote in a novel I entitled, *Green Willow*, in the thirties, and the cottage of the ancient oak tree, at which I did the bulk of my work, and now I have the bungalow of the mimosa tree. I loved the flow of the weeping willow to the ground, and I loved watching the squirrels in the old oak tree, but the mimosa tree gives me a curiously poignant pleasure when it is in flower, for mimosa is so much associated with the south of France, and that, for me, means memories of my youth. The sight of mimosa trees in flower on the French Riviera had always been so tremendously exciting, like the sight of oranges and lemons actually growing on trees. Then in the cold early English springtimes one bought mimosa at the local greengrocer's or florist's, knowing it wouldn't last in water, but it was so lovely and fragrant in its golden fluffiness for a few hours – and plunge the stems into boiling water people recommended, but I never did. During the war I published a collection of short stories under the title, *No More Mimosa*, the title symbolizing the starkness of the war years, when there was, literally, no more mimosa – or trips to the places where it still grew. Now I have a fine old mimosa tree of my own, and once it was liberated from an elm sapling that had grown in amongst it, and from strangling traveller's joy, it put on as good a show as you'd see anywhere at Hyères or Bormes-les-Mimosas. Its beauty contributed materially to the psychological aspect of settling in. Who would not happily settle-in with a big old mimosa tree? Especially when from a picture window in the sitting-room there is a middle-distance view across the river to the mountainy heights of Dartmoor? The picture window frames only a small stretch of the vast moor, the Hay Tor corner, but it frames also, on occasion, some splendid sunsets; also, when there is snow on the moor, some remarkably Alpine effects. At times the Dartmoor ridge looks grey and desolate – what Hillaby* called 'the dire moor', but it is always dramatic, for even when it is veiled in mists or hidden under banks of massed cloud, it is somehow always 'there'. Sometimes it is very near and clear, sunny and welcoming, not 'dire' at all, and in the final stage of settling-in I had a strong desire to renew acquaintance with it, to stand on those hummocks of 'tors' which I saw at all times of the day, in all weathers, from my windows.

In the spring it is a landscape-with-mimosa, here above the Teign estuary – there are some fine flowering mimosas amongst the thatched roofs in the valley – but it is all the year round a landscape with Dartmoor, forbidding or inviting, but always exciting. But first I had to renew acquaintance with the old town of Teignmouth, at the other side of the estuary, where in the spring of 1818 Keats was exasperated by the rain but enchanted by the country girls. Years ago I had seen the house in which he stayed, but now, because I was living here, my interest was proprietary. I had settled-in.

* In *Journey through Britain*, 1968.

PART II

Devon: The Local Scene

5

The Old Town of Teignmouth

Across the estuary of the river Teign, from the one-time little
fishing village of Shaldon, there is the one-time little fishing
village of Teignmouth. Shaldon is now a kind of 'select
residential' suburb of Teignmouth, and Teignmouth a
thriving holiday resort with, until recently, the remnants of
a small ship-building trade. Shaldon has a waterfront along
the river and the estuary at which small yachts and dinghies
are tied up; Teignmouth has a small harbour and quays at
which gaunt old cargo boats will collect the local clay.
Housewives from Shaldon cross the long bridge over the
estuary by 'bus into Teignmouth on shopping expeditions.
Compared with sleepy Shaldon the busy little town of
Teignmouth is almost a metropolis; going in – I quickly
discovered – 'makes a change'. Also at Teignmouth you have
the open sea, only glimpsed at Shaldon, and the open sea,
particularly on windy days, with the long white breakers
curling in, can be a very fine thing.

The 'bus terminus is the centre of the town, known as the
Triangle; it is a kind of 'circus', with shops all round, and
in the middle, islanded, public lavatories; in the mid-
nineteenth century it was a little park. At that time, too, the
grassy recreation ground on the nearby front, known as the
Den, provided grazing for sheep. Teignmouth, like Exmouth,
was fashionable as a resort as far back as the middle of the
eighteenth century.

The present town is an amalgamation of two distinct
parishes, East and West Teignmouth, and thanks to two
bombardments by the French, in the fourteenth and late

seventeenth centuries, is not older than the early eighteenth century, when it was rebuilt.

The oldest part of the town is West Teignmouth, and though it is not 'picturesque' like the Old Town of Hastings, all its timbered buildings having been destroyed by the French, it has its early eighteenth–nineteenth-century charm of narrow winding streets going down to the quays, and tall houses with the occasional bow window. There is little traffic, and there is the faded period atmosphere, shabby and with small shops, quite different from the busy, up-to-date atmosphere of the main streets of East Teignmouth.

The marine artist, Thomas Luny, built himself a house in Teign Street – then Market Street and the main street of West Teignmouth – in 1810, and died there in 1837, and Keats spent the spring of 1818 in a similar Georgian street nearby. Luny's house is now the Holiday Inn, a handsome residence with a courtyard in front and high walls on to the street.

Teignmouth has two parish churches, of which that of West Teignmouth, St James's, is the more interesting. It is generally known as the 'round church', but is in fact octagonal. It is of Norman foundation, and a tower remains, but it was rebuilt in 1819, with parts of the old church incorporated. It stands on rising ground looking out across the estuary, and G. D. and E. G. C. Griffiths in their excellent *History of Teignmouth** tell us that 'it was designed, like so many churches of its time, to serve the dual purpose of defence and worship. The slit windows in its tower were wide enough to allow snipers with bows and arrows to pick off any invaders who attempted to land west of the Tame river.' From the look-out in the belfry warning could be given of the approach of enemy ships, 'and, in all, the church was a vital part of the town's defences'. But by 1819 there was no longer need for such defences and the local gentry wanted a new church. The present building is battlemented and cumbersome, and Dr W. G. Hoskins, in what must surely be the definitive work on the county, *Devon,*† says it is 'something of a curiosity'. Baring Gould

* Brunswick Press, Teignmouth, 1965.
† 1954. Reissued by David & Charles, 1975.

called it 'hideous', and the Griffiths declare it 'in not very good taste'. Pevsner says of it is that it is 'undogmatic' – whatever that may mean as applied to architecture. I find its external oddity attractive, and it stands in a pleasant green graveyard with trees, and old tombstones ranged along a wall. It is hemmed in, now, by modern blocks of flats, but still manages to look out across the estuary. The circular interior has a blue vaulted ceiling, with stars, supported by slender iron pillars painted white, and the effect of this starry blue dome and delicate-looking white pillars is light and bright, and to my mind beautiful. Hoskins says that it makes a 'striking composition'. There is some fourteenth-century stone carving on the reredos. Despite its cumbersome exterior the interior of the church is small, which adds to its charm.

St Michael's, the parish church of East Teignmouth, stands close to the sea, just off the front, and is plain dull, late Victorian entirely, though of eleventh-century foundation. The Griffiths record that 'during the demolition of the Saxon church, three cannon balls were found embedded in the seaward walls', almost certainly relics of the French invasion of 1690. The church was rebuilt in 1823 and restored as late as 1887–9, when the tower and the western walls were rebuilt. Pevsner says of it that it is 'an almost unbelievable effort in Neo-Norman . . . entirely unworried by archaeological accuracy, and a transept front of detail as though it had been thought out by the legendary French postman'.

Before Luny built his imposing residence in Teign Street he had a house called Oak Tree House, between the stately Courtney Terrace along the front and the then grassy Triangle, and Fanny Burney stayed with her sister in a cottage in the then fishing village for three months, in July, August and September, 1773, and unlike Keats was full of praise for the town – the cleanliness of its cottages and the hardiness of its womenfolk, who did the work of men whilst their husbands were away at sea, for months at a time, engaged in the Newfoundland fishery trade.

The summer visitors to Teignmouth today will of course know East Teignmouth, with its fine promenade, with well-kept gardens, and the handsome early nineteenth century Assembly Rooms now a cinema, and its good shops, rather than shabby and rather empty old West Teignmouth, which remains still, in a sense, a separate town.

From St Michael's there is a splendid sea-wall walk along to Dawlish, under the red cliffs, skirted by the railway line – which came in 1846 – and on a clear day you can see Portland Bill shadowy in the far distance. The other way you look along the beaches to the high wooded cliff of the Ness, on the Shaldon side, at the mouth of the Teign.

In season or out Teignmouth has a feeling of life and vitality. I always liked it, and Keats might have liked to, too, if he had had better weather and been there in happier circumstances.

6

Keats was here

John Keats stayed in Teignmouth – a long stay from early
March, 1818, until early May, when he set out on the
journey back to London. The Griffiths, in their history of
Teignmouth, mention that he spent the spring of 1818 in the
town, 'in a newly-built house in the Strand, now Northumberland Place. Its exact situation is unknown.' They add
that the preface to *Endymion* is subscribed, 'Teignmouth,
April 10, 1818.' Despite the statement that the exact
situation of the house in which Keats – and his two brothers,
George and Tom – stayed is not known there is a tall old
house in Northumberland Place, a narrow, winding street
in the old part of the town leading down to the quays,
called – rightly or wrongly – Keats House, with a sign (not
a plaque) stating, starkly: The Poet Keats resided here in
1818.

Keats went down to Teignmouth from Hampstead in
order to prevent his tubercular younger brother, Tom,
who had been sent there in the belief that the climate would
benefit his health, from returning to London. Tom was
feeling better and was restless for the old London life, to
which George, also restless in Devon, had returned. John,
determined that Tom should remain, set out in the Exeter
coach, from an inn called The Swan with Two Necks, in
Lad Lane, a famous stage-coach station, at 7.30 p.m. on
3 March. The journey normally took twenty-seven hours, but
because of a violent storm the coach did not reach Exeter
until the morning of 6 March. He still had to make the last
lap of the journey to Teignmouth – which today, by 'bus

takes an hour. It is not clear from the letters* whether he continued on to Teignmouth on 6 March or on the following day, but on 13 March he wrote to his friend, Benjamin Bailey, to Magdalen Hall, Oxford, an account of his journey, and a diatribe against the county of Devon. He would appear to have arrived in Teignmouth on the 10th, for when he wrote to Bailey he had endured, already, three 'abominable' days of rain.

Benjamin Bailey was a bookish young man who was at Oxford reading for the Church. Keats had stayed with him there for some weeks during the long vacation in 1817, and regarded him as 'one of the noblest men alive'. To Bailey he wrote from Teignmouth on 13 March 1818 of his wild wet journey and of developing a cold as a result of it – he liked to ride on the outside of the coach always. He wrote of the 'abominable Devonshire weather', and declared, 'you may say what you will of Devonshire: the truth is, it is a splashy, rainy, misty snowy, foggy, haily, floody, muddy, slipshod County – the hills are very beautiful, when you get a sight of 'em – the Primroses are out, but then you are in – the Cliffs are a fine deep Colour, then the Clouds are continually vieing with them – The Women like your London People in a sort of negative way – because the native men are the poorest creatures in England. . . .' There was a great deal more of it. He fancied the 'very Air of a deteriorating quality', and thought it well that 'for the honour of Brittain Julius Caesar did not first land in this County'. He wondered that he had not met with any 'born Monsters', and concluded the tirade, 'O Devonshire, last night I thought the Moon had dwindled in heaven.'

The following day he wrote to his friend John Hamilton Reynolds, a literary young man a year older than himself. He described how the coach to Exeter had escaped being blown over in the gale, and how, 'being agog to see some Devonshire', he would have taken a walk the first day in Teignmouth, but the rain would not let him, nor on the second, third, fourth or fifth day. The letter is in the main a tirade against the weather, and recounts how he went to the theatre the other night and got insulted, though he does not

* Rollins. Vol. 1.

say in what way or by whom, but only that he did not fight and had had to date no redress. Aileen Ward, in her biography of John Keats,* suggests that 'evidently they had ladies with them', since Keats kept his temper and did not fight, but afterwards, in an angry mood, 'went doggedly ahead putting the final touches to *Endymion* and amused himself in his letters to London by blasting Devon for its "urinal qualifications" and its inhabitants as a race of "dwindled Englishmen".'

By 21 March, however, the weather had cleared up, and in a letter to his friend, Benjamin Haydon, the painter, wrote that it had been fine for three days, though it was raining that day, and he was 'coming round a bit', and had 'enjoyed the most delightful Walks' in weather 'beautiful enough to make me content here all the summer could I stay', and he enclosed some doggerel:

> *'For there's Bishop's teign*
> *And king's teign*
> *And Coomb at the clear teign head.*
> *Where close by the Stream*
> *You may have your cream*
> *All spread upon barley bread --*
>
> *There's Arch Brook*
> *And there's larch Brook*
> *Both turning many a mill*
> *And cooling the drouth*
> *Of the salmon's mouth*
> *And fattening his silver gill.'*

There is a lot more of it, but the concluding verse demands:

> *'Then who would go*
> *Into dark Soho*
> *And chatter with dack'd hair'd critics*
> *When he can stay*
> *For the new-mown hay*
> *And startle the dappled Prickets.'*

'Dack'd hair'd' is sometimes rendered 'dank-haired', but

* *John Keats, the Making of a Poet*, 1963.

Rollins* suggests 'dock-haired', short-haired, 'perhaps an oblique reference to Hazlitt'. 'Prickets', written 'thrickets' in the letter, is sometimes rendered 'crickets'. Forman† gives it as Prickets.

With this doggerel – which he called 'doggrel' – Keats also enclosed what he called some 'b—hrell', which Haydon, according to Rollins, interpreted as 'bitchrell', and which is about the Devonshire girls:‡

> *'Where be ye going you devon Maid*
> *And what have ye there i the Basket?*
> *Ye tight little fairy – just fresh from the dairy*
> *Will ye give me some cream if I ask it?*
>
> *I love you[r] Meads and I love your flowers*
> *And I love your junkets mainly*
> *But 'hind the door, I love kissing more*
> *O look no[t] so disdainly!*
>
> *I love your Hills and I love your dales*
> *And I love your flocks a bleating –*
> *But O on the hether to lie together*
> *With both our hearts a beating.*
>
> *I'll put your Basket all safe on a hook*
> *And your shawl I hang up on this willow*
> *And we will sigh in the daisy's eye*
> *And Kiss on a grass green pillow.'*

He added, 'I know not if this rhyming fit has done anything – it will be safe with you if worthy to put among my Lyrics.' He then inquired after Haydon's own work, reported that Tom had been much worse but was now getting better, and said that he had been thinking of seeing 'the dart and Plymouth'.

On 25 March Haydon replied to this that he thought the 'bi—ell, as you call it', beautiful, and expressed the hope that Keats would not leave Devonshire without going to Plymouth, 'the country around which is most exquisite . . . go round by the Totness road which is very fine, & come home by Ashburton, and then by Bridgewater where I have a

* Hyder Edward Rollins. Vol. 1. *The Letters of John Keats.* 1958
† Maurice Buxton Forman. *The Letters of John Keats.* 1935
‡ I give the Forman version, as simpler for the modern reader.

sister who will be most happy to see you.' He added that
'Devonshire has somehow or other the character of being
rainy, but I must own to you that I do not think it is more
so than any other County, and pray remember the time of
year; it has rained in Town almost incessantly ever since
you went away, the fact is you dog you carry the rain with
you as Ulysses did the Winds and then opening your rain
bags you look round with a knowing wink, and say "curse
this Devonshire how it rains!" Stay till the Summer, and
then bask in its deep blue summer Sky, and lush grass, &
tawny banks, and silver bubbling rivers – you must not leave
Devonshire without seeing some of its Scenery, rocky,
mossy, craggy with roaring rivers & as clear as crystal – it
will do your mind good – '

Keats did not get to Plymouth, though promised to return
'at some more favourable time of the year' to visit Devon
'thoroughly', but he did get to the fair at Dawlish and wrote
to his friend James Rice, in London, recording the visit in
verse:

> '*Over the hill and over the dale,*
> *And over the bourne to Dawlish –*
> *Where Gingerbread wives have a scanty sale*
> *And gingerbre[ad] nuts are smallish.*'

He evidently encountered a willing girl there, for the
doggerel continues:

> '*Rantipole Betty she ran down a hill*
> *And ki[c]k'd up her pettic[o]ats fairly*
> *Says I I'll be Jack if you will be Gill.*
> *So she sat on the Grass debonnairly.*'

After which

> '. . . *without any fuss any hawing and humming*
> *She lay on the grass debonnai[r]ly.*'

There were evidently people about for she complained of
'somebody here and somebody there' but he ordered her to
hold her tongue –

> '*So she held her tongue and lay plump and fair*
> *And dead as a venus tipsy.*'

He concludes the episode in an excruciatingly bad verse:

> '*O who wouldn't hie to Dawlish fair*
> *O who wouldn't stop in a Meadow*
> *O [who] would not rumple the daisies there*
> *And make the wild fern for a bed do.*'

Keats would have walked the short distance along by the sea and over the cliffs to Dawlish, but to reach the Arch bridge he mentioned in his 'doggrel' to Haydon he would have had to have crossed the river and walked along the estuary towards Newton Abbot, and as the bridge had not been built at that time (the first wooden bridge, then the longest in England, was not built until 1827, by which time Keats had been dead five years) he would have had to get a boatman, probably a fisherman, to take him across to the then fishing village of Shaldon. At the end of the eighteenth century, the Griffiths tell us, there were three jetties at Shaldon, used for landing fish, and Coombe Cellars – just beyond the Arch bridge, and now a pleasant pub – was believed to have been a salting place. The Arch bridge is a small stone bridge over a stream which flows out into the estuary, marshy at that point, with a milestone indicating Coombe village just beyond. It is only a short walk from Shaldon. The Griffiths tell us that by 1817, that is to say when Keats was there, Teignmouth had a population of about 4000, and its streets were 'narrow and stank of stale fish'; its leading citizens were 'merchants and sea-captains engaged in voyages to Spain, the Mediterranean, Newfoundland and Labrador'. There is still a part of the cliff, off the Torquay road, known as Labrador.

Keats would have been able to post his letters in West Teignmouth at a small post-office from which the mail went out by coach every day at 6 p.m. The incoming mail, the Griffiths write, arrived at 7 p.m. and was delivered next morning. The Royal Express coach left Exeter at 4 p.m. and reached Teignmouth at 7 p.m., coming via Dawlish – as the 'bus today does, but the 'bus make the journey in an hour.

On 25 March Keats wrote a letter in the form of a poem to Reynolds, written in melancholy mood, and it is in this poem that he writes of walking along the sands and looking 'too far into the sea', where he saw how 'the greater on the less feeds evermore', and saw 'too distinct into the core/Of an eternal fierce destruction'. He had gathered 'young spring leaves, and flowers gay/Of Periwinkle and wild strawberry', but he had also seen a hawk pounce, and a robin 'ravening a worm', and the cruelty of nature oppressed his spirit. He concluded the letter in prose, mentioning that 'The Rain is come on again', and adding, 'I think with me Devonshire stands a very poor chance, I shall damn it up hill and down dale, if it keeps up to the average of 6 fine days in three weeks'.

He wrote again to Reynolds on 9 April, reporting that 'Devonshire continues rainy', and that he had not been able to visit 'Kents' Ca[ve]' at Babbicun', but had on one very beautiful day 'a fine Clamber over the rocks all along as far as that place'. That was a considerable walk, but he was at that time, before the tuberculosis took a hold of him, a considerable walker, as the record of his walks in Scotland with his great friend Charles Brown reveals.

On 10 April he wrote again to Reynolds, sending the Preface to *Endymion*, which he hoped his friend would find 'tolerable', complaining again about the weather. 'The Climate here weighs us down completely,' he wrote. 'Tom is quite low spirited.' He added, 'I wanted to send you a few songs written in your favourite Devon – it cannot be – Rain! Rain! Rain!' Nevertheless he had gone out the previous day and 'found a lane bank'd at each side with store of Primroses, whilst the earlier bushes are beginning to leaf'.

He did not write again to Reynolds until 27 April, and he had then lain awake last night 'listening to the Rain with a sense of being drowned and rotted like a grain of wheat', but Tom had 'taken a fancy' to a local physician and seemed to be getting better, and they might therefore remain for some months – they in fact left for London on 4 or 5 May, going by Honiton and Bridport. He wrote to Reynolds from Teignmouth for the last time on 3 May, and was looking forward to summer days with Tom on Hampstead Heath, as in the previous summer. He writes at length and manages not to mention the weather, but only that the leaves have been out in Devon for many a day.

From Honiton Keats wrote to his Teignmouth landlady, Mrs Margaret Jeffrey, that Tom had borne the journey thus far 'remarkably well'. He sent their goodbyes again to the two daughters, Marianne and Fanny, to whom all the Keats brothers (for George rejoined John and Tom) had been attracted. There were in fact three daughters, but it was with the two elder ones, 'laughing thoughtless Sarah' and 'steady quiet Marianne', that George and Tom had been flirtatious, though it was with John that Marianne had fallen in love and to whom she poured out her heart in sentimental verse which was later published with her other verse. Keats, preoccupied with Tom's health, and his work on *Endymion*, had too much on his mind to respond. The poor girl suffered when the Keats brothers left Teignmouth, and the poem *Si deseris pereo*, in her published book of verse, is supposed to have been written to John:

> '*If thou canst bear to say adieu,*
> *To her who loves so warm, so true;*
> *If thou canst think thou mayst depart,*
> *Yet leave unbroken the young heart,*
> *Which gave to thee its earliest vow*
> *And lives but in thy presence now;*
> *Then quit thy love, thy bride – but know*
> *Si deseris, ah, pereo.*'

There is a lot more in a similar strain, but she does say that 'the pang will be Soon o'er', and she in due course married, and published her poetry under her married name, Mrs I. S. Prowse.

Endymion was published immediately on Keats's return to London, and he was never again in Devonshire – but he did get to see Kent's Cavern before he left, walking all along the coast to it, and his two months in Teignmouth were not a dead loss, despite the weather and Tom's deteriorating health, any more than they were all a nonsense of disarrayed petticoats and the pulled apron-strings of dairy-maids – in fact he wrote a last Teignmouth letter to Reynolds on 3 May in which he referred to 'Venery' as 'a bestial or joyless thing';

no man, he wrote, could set it down until he was 'sick of it',
and it is clear from the philosophic content of the letter that
he himself was. The whole long letter is in a serious, philosophic vein, far removed from the fooling of the 'doggrel' and
'bitchrell' he had sent Haydon two months earlier. He was
working on *Endymion* and had begun *Isabella*, and had
looked deeply into the sea – 'too far into the sea', but it was
the beginning of understanding of poetry in relation to life –
of which he had only three more years left, and Tom very
much less. Looking into the sea from the rocky Teignmouth
shore he saw imagination 'brought beyond its proper
bound, yet still confined, Lost in a sort of Purgatory blind',
and unable to refer to 'any standard law of earth or heaven'.
The experience was all part of the making of the great poet
he was to become; he had still to write *Hyperion* and his
wonderful Odes, and by then he was far gone in what he
called, and which in fact was, the 'family disease', tuberculosis.

7

Cockington Court

When Teignmouth was at the height of its popularity as a watering place, between 1820 and 1828, Torquay was still a small unmapped fishing village, but within thirty years it was to become known as 'the Queen of Watering Places' and 'the Montpellier of England', and its growth stimulated by the coming of the railway in 1848. But even before the railway it had become fashionable, renowned for its mild winters, and an elegant town catering for the quality. Dr Hoskins cites a book published in 1832, *A Panorama of Torquay*, by Octavian Blewitt, in which the author 'tells us, among other things, that those who wished to avoid the fatigue of the long coach journey from London, travelled to Portsmouth by coach and there took the *Brunswick* – "a steam vessel of considerable power" direct to Torquay.'

The history of Torquay, as recounted by Dr Hoskins, is interesting: Torre Abbey built a small quay there in medieval times, and Tor Bay was used by the English fleet in the seventeenth and eighteenth centuries in preference to Plymouth Sound, which was more exposed. The fleet anchored there for long periods during the Napoleonic Wars, and the wives and families of officers were brought down to Tor Quay and accommodation found for them ashore in the existing hamlet, so that it developed, though by 1821 the population was still under 2000. By 1841 it was nearly 6000, 'and some elegant terraces were being built', but 'the period of most rapid growth was between 1841 and 1871 . . . and this has stamped Torquay architecturally as a mid-Victorian town'.

The great charm – and uniqueness – of Torquay, of
course, lies in the way in which the town rises in terraces on
the hillsides round an inner harbour, so that one is reminded
of Cannes. The palm trees in the gardens along the promenade add to this French Riviera atmosphere. Much of the
splendid lay-out of Torquay is due to the nineteenth-century
Sir Lawrence Palk, a big landowner, who began the construction of the inner harbour and built terraces of houses on
the hillsides as 'lodging houses for genteel families'. The town
was developed to cater for the well-to-do, so that it is ironic
that in the late twentieth century it is as popular in the
summer with 'hippies' as is St Ives in Cornwall. Sir Lawrence
would, as they say, turn in his grave – as would the Mallocks
of Cockington, who did not want a town here at all on the
threshold of their fine estate a mile or so inland from the
sea, and threw away a fortune, says Dr Hoskins, rather than
have it. 'Not until 1865 did one of them consent to grant a
building lease, and that only to a family connection.' The
Mallocks acquired Cockington Court from the Cary family
in 1654, and it remained with them until 1927. In 1935 the
house and park were acquired by the Torquay Corporation.
Pevsner agrees that 'the grounds in which lie Cockington
Court – "built by the Carys and classicized by the Mallocks"
– Cockington Church, and the Drum Inn are beautifully
kept by the Corporation of Torquay and make an extremely
pleasing picture', but adds, snootily, that it has all become
'a standard afternoon trip for visitors to Torquay, and there
is complete harmony between the sight-seeing townsman,
the cottages ready to be admired, and the Drum Inn by
Lutyens, 1934'.

It is true that the village of Cockington, with its too-well-
kept thatched cottages, its old forge, its water-wheel, is over
picturesque, self-consciously so, and the addition of souvenir
shops makes it an 'unreal' place – too much a show place
catering for the summer tourists, who may arrive at, and
depart from it, by horse-drawn carriages, but the fact also
remains that Cockington Court, and the superbly kept small
park in which it stands, are extremely beautiful.

The house stands in a hollow, with great lawns sweeping
down to it, and the lovely little church, poised above it a

short distance off. It is the church of St George and St Mary, fourteenth and fifteenth century, though the tower is thirteenth, and there is some medieval glass. According to a leaflet available in the church it began as a chapel, forty-nine feet by fourteen, in 1070–80, and was acquired by Torre Abbey in 1236, soon after which the tower was built. Sir George Cary is buried with his daughters in the church, and there is a Mallock window. The font is fifteenth century, the pulpit 'probably Tudor'; the altar rails Jacobean, restored in 1901. The beautiful barrel roof is a replica made in 1950, the original having been partially destroyed by bomb blast in 1943. The tower was re-roofed as late as 1965. Despite these restorations, however, the feeling of the little church is one of great antiquity, and it has, in fact, stood there for nearly a thousand years. The pulpit is very beautiful, with lovely carvings. Pevsner says that it is 'the most interesting piece in the church'. It was brought from Torre Church in 1825, when Torquay was still a village.

There are some magnificent old trees round the church, and in the hollow below, behind the beautiful old house, there are walled rose-gardens. From the point of view of the de Cockingtons, the Carys, and the Mallocks, who between them held the manor of Cockington for over eight hundred years, the fact that the ground floor of Cockington Court is now a tea-room during the holiday season is a terrible come-down, but for the hoi-polloi of the late twentieth century it is very pleasant.

A short walk along wooded paths, past a heather garden, brings one to two small lakes in a setting of rhododendrons and azaleas, eucalyptus trees and camellias. The woods slope down to the water, and there are varieties of ducks, and at any time of the year, in all seasons, and even in a drizzling rain, as I have seen it, this is a very beautiful spot. If the thatched lodge with its Gothic windows, and its verandah supported by tree trunks, is just plain silly, never mind – there are joys to come. Before I saw Dartington Hall I thought Cockington Court and its grounds as beautiful a place of its kind as I would ever behold; it is still a very favourite place with me, but once you have seen Dartington Hall you are spoiled for anything else. . . .

8

Dartington Hall

Back in the 'twenties, when I first met, and was excited by
the educational ideas of, A. S. Neill, 'Dartington Hall' was
merely the name of an expensive co-educational 'pro-
gressive' school run by an American couple, Leonard
Elmhirst and his wife. Neill was impatient of it as a
'millionaire's school', and he was not interested in 'pro-
gressive' educational ideas but only in the 'free' school –
complete freedom in education, as exemplified in his own
school, Summerhill, then at Lyme Regis in Dorset. That was
in 1925, the year in which the Elmhirsts acquired Dartington
Hall, restored it, started the school, and a considerable rural
enterprise on a thousand acres of land. None of this interested
me at the time, being then interested only in Neill's revolutionary educational ideas, and sharing his impatience of
anything less in the educational field.

I maintain, to this day, my interest in, and support of,
Neill's educational radicalism, but the degree of 'pro-
gressiveness' of Dartington Hall School has become irrelevant; that it is a fine school, specializing in music, I am sure,
and certainly the Dartington Hall rural project, with its
farm, tweed-making, pottery, glass, saw-mills, and much
else, is remarkable. Dr Hoskins calls it 'a remarkable
experiment in rural reconstruction', and the restoration of
the Hall itself was a noble enterprise.

What interests me today is the architectural wonder of
what Pevsner calls 'the most spectacular medieval mansion
of Devon'. It is fourteenth century and grey, and is approached from a large grassy quadrangle with cherry trees,

which, in bloom, set off the beauty of the grey stone. From a gatehouse, with outside steps leading up to the living quarters, extend a row of old grey houses that were once the servants' and retainers' dwellings, and the Great Hall is a vast barn with a lofty timbered roof, with fine vaulted entrance porch with Richard II's White Hart as the centre boss. Beyond this quite wonderful medieval building there is a tilt yard, now used as an Open Air Theatre, with huge and amazingly clipped yew trees, and tiers of immaculately mown grassy banks, all surrounded by woodlands full of flowers, and the whole in a setting of undulating pastureland. From the far side of the Open Theatre, flanked by a row of twisted ancient trees, the grey buildings of the Hall are a dream of beauty – a dream for me abruptly broken a few paces farther on by the grotesque hulk of a Henry Moore sculpture of a Reclining Woman. Surely something classically graceful should have occupied that site? But either you are modern-minded where art is concerned or you are not, and I am not.

When you descend steps through the tall heather bushes, from the top of the Open Air Theatre, you can follow a path to the Garden Centre, and on the way pass a charming sculpture of a donkey, dated 1934; this also is 'modern', but a world away from Henry Moore.

The modern school buildings blend remarkably well into the landscape; they are of the 'thirties and are thus not too aggressively 'functional' in their setting – though one always looks away from them and back to the medieval splendour.

Only the tower of the old church of Dartington, St Mary's, which stood beside the Hall, remains standing. The church was demolished in 1873, and rebuilt beside the main Totnes road, and completed in 1880. It was rebuilt in replica, and much of the materials of the old church used, including the font, pulpit, roof, and chancel screen; the south porch also contains fragments and fittings from the old church.

Of Dartington village one sees very little when visiting Dartington Hall – it lies huddled a way outside the thousand-acre estate, in a bend of the river Dart, and dates from the twelfth century. The Dart Valley is very beautiful here, and the little railway line winds through it, beside the river. There is a little steam train, like a toy train, which comes snaking out of the woods, sounding its whistle importantly as it puffs along. One coach is labelled Great Western, another Devon Belle, another Buffet, and with its brightly shining brass and its curling steam it makes a charming sight. I was reminded of the little Worth Valley train at Haworth, which was used in the much-praised film, *The Railway Children*. Like that it is a kind of 'Bluebell Line' train, 'playing trains', but it is a pleasant game, and one of the better tourist attractions.

Dartington is just beyond the attractive old town of Totnes, and coming by road from Teignmouth there is a fine view of the town, with the castle on its mound. It was from the ramparts of Totnes Castle that I had my first view of Dartington Hall, 'on its wooded hill above the river', as I wrote,* in 1969, but I was only mildly interested – 'Oh, yes, the famous school!' I was assured it was very beautiful, and the grounds. No one told me that it was *incredibly* beautiful. I am happy to pass on the news.

But for whom was it all created? It's a fair question, and I asked it myself. I am indebted to Dr Hoskins for the following facts, for Dartington Hall is not a show place but a serious agricultural–industrial–educational enterprise, and they do not issue a tourist's handbook about themselves. But Dr Hoskins tells us that Dartington was 'part of the possessions of the Martins from the early twelfth century onwards', and that after about eight generations the Martin estates escheated to the crown, and in 1384 Richard II granted Dartington and other lands to his brother, John Holland, who became the Duke of Exeter in 1397. The Duke made Dartington his principal seat in Devon and created the great Hall. 'After various changes of ownership the manor came to Sir Arthur Champernowne (died 1578) who made the extensive alterations to the house which may still be seen.' In Georgian times further changes were made. The Champernownes held the manor until the twentieth century, 'but parts of the Hall were allowed to fall into ruin'. It was this ruin the Elmhirsts so courageously took over in 1925. Pevsner says that 'it may be objected that the fourteenth-century Dartington has re-emerged almost too perfect from under the hands

* In *England at Large*, 1970.

of the careful and wealthy restorers', adding that the setting and buildings 'certainly combine the genuine with the liveable-in to a degree which must appear even more ideal to the American than to the sloppier British'.

And Pevsner considers the reclining figure by Henry Moore 'splendid'.

9

'The Dire Moor'

I use Hillaby's phrase because it encapsulates my own feeling
about the high moor, which I see from my windows every
day and always find dramatic, and sometimes beautiful, but
at heart I am afraid of it. Moors frighten me, as deserts do.
Like deserts they seem to go on forever, and there is always
the feeling that if you left the road, or the path, you would be
irretrievably lost. There are people who find deserts romantic; for me they have always been terrifyingly lonely,
desolate wildernesses; and that goes for moors, too. When I
was writing *England My Adventure*,* in which I associated
places with people, I went to Haworth, and viewing the vast
moorland flowing down to the Brontë parsonage, laving it
like a great brown sea, I could only think how terrible to
live there, with all that at one's back door, but Emily,
especially, loved it, wrote poems about it, and was desperately unhappy when removed from it . . . so much so that
she had to be brought back. Charlotte wrote to Mrs Gaskell,
in 1853, urging her to come soon, for the heather was in
bloom on the moors; she told her, also, that Emily was 'never
happy or well but on the sweeping moors that gathered
round her home', and she and Emily walked a good deal on
the moors, 'to the great damage of our shoes'. Mrs Gaskell,
too, was fascinated by the moors. 'August', she wrote, 'was
the season of glory for the neighbourhood of Haworth. Even
the smoke, lying in the valley between the village and
Keighley, took beauty from the radiant colours on the moors
above. . . .' Ellen Nussey, Charlotte's life-long friend, also

* 1972

wrote glowingly of the happiness of the Brontë girls out on
the moors, 'nothing appearing in view but miles and miles
of heather'.

Chacun à son goût. Also, that is all very well in high summer,
but in the winter there is no splendour of purple heather
and golden gorse, only the boggy brown wilderness flowing
away to infinity. I never felt this desolation in the Irish bogs –
I think because the Irish bog landscape is always broken up
by the stacks of turf, and by the stray white cabin – as in
the Paul Henry paintings. The bogs roll away to the horizon,
but they are well-crossed by roads and paths; they are
somehow not desolate, or endowed with what Hillaby calls
'environmental hostility', as moors are. Anyhow for me.

Hillaby says that Dartmoor is 'the hard core of Devon'.
He says, also, that it is a dome, and 'from a distance looks
like an enormous teacake with a flat top and rounded sides'.
It doesn't look at all like that to me, from my house, but like a
mountain ridge, with hummocks of tors, Hay Tor, which is
two hummocks, like the 'breasts' of the Jungfrau mountain
in Austria. On a clear day the ridge is blue and beautiful;
under snow it looks Alpine. A good deal of the time it is
misty, and hostile with desolateness.

But at weekends in the 'season' the beauty spots and
viewing points on Dartmoor, the 'honey pots', as they are
called, are thick with cars and people, and they say that
there is barely standing room on Hay Tor. . . . But for all
this I have met other people who share my own sense of the
'environmental hostility' of moors.

I have been up to Hay Tor in good weather and scrambled
amongst the high, massive rocks, but the day I saw the
delicate grey beauty of Dartington Hall in sunshine, all
cherry blossom against ancient grey stone, I saw Dartmoor
under snow. It was another world, with even a different
climate.

I do not know what the weather was like at Dartington
that afternoon, whether the morning's sunshine retreated into
greyness, but certainly there was no snow; snow was what we
drove into as we headed north to Princetown, though
Buckfast, with cars milling around the Abbey, and Dartmeet
with its 'clapper bridge', which is a pack-horse bridge of

slabs of flat stone laid on stone pillars, following the little river Dart, and at Staverton Bridge, grey and beautiful, sixteenth century, crossing the Dart Valley railway line, at a station little more than a halt, where the train had ended its journey, and on to the Two Bridges Hotel, where again there were cars, for this is a 'honey pot'.

At Two Bridges you leave the main road and follow a secondary road to the grim little town which Pevsner says is 'unquestionably the bleakest place of Devon', the prison town which is Princetown. As you drive into it you see the grim contours of the prison on your left, shadowy that afternoon because of the mist and the persistent snow. Princetown is over fourteen hundred feet high, and exposed on all sides, and nobody would live there, you feel, if they didn't have to – that is to say unless they were associated in some way with the prison. You notice, as you drive in, a Prison Officers' Club, and an Officers' Mess. There is a small hotel and a nineteenth-century church. It seems extraordinary that in the late eighteenth century a gentleman called Sir Thomas Tyrwhitt, Lord Warden of the Stannaries and a friend of the then Prince of Wales, should elect to build himself a house in so bleak a spot, but this he did, and called it Tor Royal, in honour of the prince. Tyrwhitt wanted a house near his granite quarries, and he had, also, an idea of opening up Dartmoor, and thus conceived the idea of building barracks at that point to house prisoners of the Napoleonic wars, who could be employed to build roads. This was the beginning of Dartmoor prison. The barracks were begun in 1806, occupying an area of thirty acres. There were five buildings, of two storeys each, of which only one is supposed to survive, known as the French prison. The place became a prison settlement in 1850, but the town grew up around the original prisoners-of-war barracks, and was named after the Prince, who gave the site. He held all the lands of the Duchy of Cornwall, to which all Dartmoor belonged. The Duchy Hotel, rebuilt, like Tor Royal, still exists. Who, I wonder, stays in it? Visiting prison officials? No one goes to Princetown for fun. Dr Hoskins calls it 'a grim little town. . . . with an abominable climate of fog, snow, wind, and more than 80 inches of cold rain – sometimes over

100. It stands on a *col* between the two Hessary Tors, exposed to the bitter north and east winds, the least suitable place that could ever have been chosen for a town.' But here, apparently, Sir Thomas Tyrwhitt made a 'productive estate', and was the originator of the good roads that now cross the Moor, and notably the road from Tavistock to Princetown. With the closing of the prison in 1816, Dr Hoskins tells us, the town almost collapsed, 'but the completion of the Dartmoor Railway in 1823 brought back many people to the granite quarries'. The prison remained derelict until 1850, when it was re-opened for long-term prisoners. I was interested to note that cars are forbidden to stop along the wooded road leading to the prison.

The author of a sardonic little book, *How to Survive in the Nick*,* wrote of his personal experience of Dartmoor prison, 'Cold, dismal, damp, far away. A god-forsaken hole that just doesn't care if you live or die. Lots of outside work if you only have a short time left. Princetown exists only because of the prison. The locals either work in the nick or sell tourists mementoes of the bygone days when the prison was full of French and American prisoners of war (dating back to the American Civil War). Visitors from London should allow two days for travel.'

It was not all grim on the road to Princetown. There are wooded beauty spots, with old bridges and the Dart tumbling over boulders, but in the main the moor rolls away into the distance at either side of the road, and for the most part it is like crossing a desert, though in other places, with stone walls striping the moor up into dun meadows, it is reminiscent of the West of Ireland. There are the numerous rocky hillocks or tors, and occasional collections of huge stones, like Stonehenge, which have been pre-historic huts and other Bronze Age remains. But on that wintry March day my chief impression was of the moor flowing away to the horizon like a great empty sea, and of high lonely tors lost in mist – Dartmoor at its most 'dire' . . . which was how Hillaby experienced it.

It was interesting to have seen it like that, at its worst, but I felt that to form a proper impression of it I must also

* By Jonathan Marshal, 1975.

eats House, Northumberland Place, Teignmouth

St Nicholas Church, Ringmore, Shaldon

Cockington Church, with Cockington Hall

see it at its best, in sunshine. But unless you are going to write an entire book about the great moor, like Brian Crossing's classic *Guide to Dartmoor,** all that it is possible to record in a single chapter in a book like this are a few general impressions. Dartmoor is too vast and too varied to be conveyed adequately in a short space.

I was to see Dartmoor again in brilliant May sunshine, and then many aspects of it were revealed as very attractive – and even Princetown did not seem all that grim, though spring had not caught up there, with the beech trees, in full leaf down below, up there still only in brown bud. I was interested, this time, to see Tyrwhitt's house, Tor Royal, buried in trees some way out of the town, and laved by the brown sea of the moor. There is very little habitation in this part of the moor, and even the vegetation is only rough grass and heather, a lonely and desolate place in which to build a fine house, but Tyrwhitt, as we know, had to be near his granite quarries.

The route from Lower Dean via Buckfastleigh and the National Trust woodlands of Hembury to Princetown is very beautiful, the moor wooded and hilly, and threaded by narrow lanes with over-arching trees and, in May, banks of bluebells. There is gorse everywhere in this area, burnishing the moor most spectacularly. After leaving Poundsgate, a small village of stone-built cottages and thatched roofs, the moor is no longer wooded but all bare rolling hills, with outcrops of tors and occasional clumps of firs. The road descends to Dartmeet, which is a beauty spot, and therefore a 'honey pot' with cars and people, then climbs up again to wild, bare moorland, with a row of tors on a ridge and a distant view of Princetown, with a television aerial on a hilltop dominating it – invisible on my previous visit because of the mists of snow. The grim buildings of the prison are plainly discernible – and the May sunshine can do nothing to alleviate that grimness. We come to Two Bridges, with its hotel, and there are groups of walkers with scarlet packs on their backs, there are ewes and lambs galore, and shaggy ponies grazing the roadsides, where the grass is greener.

* First published in 1912. Re-issued in 1965, with a new introduction by Brian Le Messurier, by David and Charles. Subsequent editions.

C

At Burrator, another 'honey pot', there are beech woods, and a 'guided walk' centre, and the reservoir which looks like a Scottish lock, with the woods going down to it and a peninsula jutting out into it with the effect of a wooded island. This reservoir supplies the water for Plymouth and is served by a leat – a narrow, canalized stream – which seemed to have followed us all the way, but which is most in evidence at Swincombe, where it crosses the wide, wild valley where a reservoir was to have been made but was prevented by public protest.

Motorists from Plymouth flock to Cadover Bridge, over the little river Plym, and on the descent to it there are distant views of Plymouth and a blue line that is the sea. There are here the first clay-workings, which at Lee Moor, a little farther on, offer a white lunar landscape, and powder the fir trees and shrubs a short distance from them with white, as though they had been caught in a snow shower. There is the almost blinding white of the deep clay pits and the steep clay hills, and the soft blue horizon that is the sea. The clay-workings are not beautiful; they are even disfiguring, but they are spectacular, and should be seen.

As should such 'obvious' places as the almost chronically picturesque little stannary town of Chagford, and the tourist-trap that is the undeniably attractive little village of Widecombe-in-the-Moor. I revisited both on a third visit to Dartmoor in the spring of 1975 and was glad to renew the acquaintance. I was taken on that occasion via Chudleigh, through the densely wooded and extremely beautiful Teign Valley. From the little market town of Moretonhampstead there is the climb up to the moor – some eight hundred feet – which in late May means bluebells again, though they are finished down below, and slopes shining with gorse. There are roughly built stone walls, very reminiscent of Connemara, striping the moorland up into fields, and at one point on the road to Chagford there is a fine view across the valley to the twentieth-century Castle Drogo, which Pevsner calls an 'extravaganza in granite'. It was designed by Lutyens for Mr J. C. Drewe, of Drewsteignton, who had made a fortune in the grocery business and wanted not merely a country house but a castle. It was begun in 1911 and completed in 1930, and Hoskins calls it 'one of Lutyens' less-known masterpieces', and says of it is that it is 'the last castle to be built in England and perhaps the last private building in granite'. He considers that the massed effect is 'overwhelming'. Certainly it looks very fine in its setting of trees on the slopes of the moor, with Exmoor in the blue distance behind, and the river below. Its predominant style is Tudor, and it was named after the Drogo who was lord of the manor at the time of Richard I. It is open to the public – admission fee 80 pence. I have no desire to visit it, not approving of twentieth-century castles, but people who have done so assure me it is 'fascinating'.

Chagford stands on a hill a thousand feet above the Teign Valley in a very beautiful moorland setting, with glimpses of the moorland slopes rising at the end of narrow streets, sealing them off. It has a fifteenth-century granite church, St Michael's, with a fine tower, and a number of sixteenth-century granite houses with thatched roofs, the most attractive of which is perhaps the Church Stile Cottage, facing the church. Close to it is the picturesque Three Crowns Hotel, thatched and with mullioned windows, and the Ring o' Bells pub with its Ringers' Beer Garden. There is a Market Cross in the square, just below the church, much restored, according to Pevsner, where the old stone horse troughs are now used for flowers. After its decline as a tinners' town, at the end of the sixteenth century, Chagford developed a woollen industry and became, also, increasingly important as a market town until the late nineteenth century. Today it is a somewhat select moorland holiday resort, with expensive shops and a generally well-heeled air.

The church is grey granite inside, with a barrel roof with gilded bosses, and painted altar screens. The centre boss of the chancel roof shows the tinners' sign of three rabbits. All the pillars in the nave are made from single blocks of granite; there is some good wood carving, and a blue and gold Lady chapel. I was interested in a tablet by the door which described the custom of distributing 'One Pound Seven Shillings worth of Bread, called Bonamus Bread', to 'the Poor of this Parish'. It was distributed by the churchwardens every Good Friday, and the custom was 'to be continued forever'.

Another notice concerned the education of Six Poor Children, who were to be taught Reading, Writing and Arithmetic, and two of whom were to be duly apprenticed to a trade. A little I resented those tablets with their complacent patronage of The Poor, the virtuousness recorded in stone for posterity in the parish church.

There is some modern work in the church, a painted screen by a Devon artist, Herbert Read; and there is a processional cross made from the aluminium of the first Zeppelin to be brought down in England in 1916. Altogether a very interesting church.

I had been a little doubtful about revisiting Widecombe. It could only be, I thought, after so many years, more touristic than ever. Whether or not it is I don't really know, though touristic it certainly is, with its souvenir shops, postcards, clotted cream, Devonshire honey, litter-strewn car-park accommodating the big white tourist coaches, and Ye Olde Glebe House (*circa* 1527) with its placard urging visitors to 'See the Dartmoor fireplace and Tom Cobley's chair'. There is a village sign depicting 'Uncle Tom Cobley and all' on the grey mare jogging off to Widecombe Fair, setting the stamp of self-consciousness on the place; but when all that is acknowledged Widecombe is still a very attractive Dartmoor village, with a good deal of interest. A feature of the square, which has Glebe House at one side and the old Church House at the other, with the church completing the group, is the old yew tree and the pollarded elm, side by side, ringed round at the base with stone. It was these trees which I had remembered when I had forgotten all else about Widecombe except a vague picturesqueness. The old Church House is sixteenth century, grey granite, and now the property of the National Trust. With its loggia it is like the almshouses which are the chief feature of Moreton-hampstead. Across the square from it is the Glebe House, grey stone and thatch, and the pinnacled tower of the church – the 'cathedral of the moor' – which is, as Brian Watson says in his *Shell Guide*, 'nearly as splendid as Magdalen Tower, Oxford'. He adds that it was probably built by the tin miners 'to surpass the neighbouring, but distant, parish churches'. Hoskins tells us that the pinnacles of the tower are 'very characteristic of church towers around Dartmoor'.

The interior of the church – St Pancras – is light and bright, with a vaulted barrel roof, and the remains of early sixteenth-century painted screens of saints, and in the entrance porch tablets recounting in verse how the church was struck by lightning during a service on 21 October 1538 when four people were killed and sixty-two injured, though the clergyman author of these rustic verses seems to have regarded the whole episode as an example of the mercy of God, in that many people whose clothing was scorched, even to one man having the money in his purse melted, nevertheless survived.

The moor enclosing Widecombe is spectacular with great boulders and outcrops of rock, and there is the feeling of the village being at the very heart of Dartmoor.

Beyond it lies a Forestry Commission area with dense plantations of firs, and there are the remains of a clapper bridge, its middle slab swept away, though it is difficult to imagine the babbling little East Dart ever becoming a raging torrent. There are here green fields of reclaimed moorland, with grazing cattle, and all is serene and gentle, and the air sweet with the warm scent of gorse. Here is Dartmoor at its most sylvan, utterly remote from the wildness and emptiness of the Princetown area, the trackless wastes of Hillaby's 'dire moor'.

At its most sylvan, too, is the moor at Fingle Bridge, which I saw in the late autumn, with the wooded slopes goldening down to the river Teign, a stream tumbling over boulders, though only some twenty-five miles from its wide estuary. There is a pub here, with log fires and a restaurant. The grey granite bridge is Elizabethan and designed for pack-horses, and, as Crossing says, 'the visitor here will find himself in the midst of some of the most charming and romantic scenery in the Westcountry'. The nearest village is Drewsteignton, small and grey and picturesque, at one time remote, but now linked to the outer world by a 'bus service.

Continuing on through the wooded lands to Hound Tor you come to a small cross-roads and a mound uncommonly like a grave, and it is, in fact Jay's Grave, reputedly the grave of a suicide, Kitty Jay, a young unmarried woman who hanged herself in a barn, and who, as Crossing says, 'in accordance with the barbarous custom of the times was interred at this cross-way'. Crossing offers no reason for her suicide, but says only that 'more than forty years ago' – he wrote at the end of the nineteenth century – 'Mr James Bryant, of Hedge Barton, caused the grave to be opened, when human bones, including a skull, were discovered and declared on examination to be those of a female. The date of the unfortunate woman's death is unknown, as no one then remembered the occurrence. Mr Bryant had the bones placed in a box and re-interred on the spot where they had been found, and raised the mound and set up the stones that now mark it.' The stones are very simple; there is no cross; but there are always flowers on the mound, I am told, and no one knows who places them there. The day I was there two small containers held a sprig of spruce and piece of rhododendron. The local version of the story is that poor Kitty Jay was pregnant and deserted by her lover. Oddly, of the many books about Dartmoor, only Crossing mentions Jay's Grave.

The mound is at the edge of Hound Tor Down, and here the moor becomes wild again. The rocks of Hound Tor are huge, and the effect across the moor is of a high ridge, which some see as in the shape of a hound, but which seemed to me only a rocky island in the wild empty sea of the moor.

I have still not seen the moor at its wildest, in the north, in the Okehampton area, but have no wish to. Give me the beech woods and the 'honey pots' every time, people and cars and all. From various points guided walks may be taken, and on a guided walk no harm can come, yet I know that for myself once I had stepped off the road into that vast brown and green sea of moorland the irrational fear of environmental hostility would seize me – the dread of being engulfed. . . .

10

Writers in Devon

It is interesting that, wild and dramatic as it is, Dartmoor has, as Hoskins points out, 'produced no literature or poetry of the highest order. No Hardy or Brontë has ever felt its power and translated it into mortal words.' He adds that Devonshire 'has been a playground rather than a workshop for writers'. Fanny Burney spent several weeks in Teignmouth in the summer of 1773 and was full of praise for the beauties of Devon, but visiting Exeter in 1788 she found it 'close and ugly'. Three years later she was in Sidmouth and Exmouth, and from the latter crossed the river Teign to Starcross, where the was shocked by the sight of women with legs 'entirely naked' gathering cockles. Devon, in spite of the initial impact of beauty, made no lasting impression on her, any more than it did on Shelley, who spent ten weeks at Lynmouth, but had little or nothing to say about the scenery. Hardy knew parts of Devon well, but, says Hoskins, 'apart from one or two passing references in his novels and poetry, he speaks of Devon not at all'. He suggests that Devon is too soft in its beauty – he uses the word 'feminine' – to inspire great poetry, that it 'lacks austerity and the elements of nobility and sadness'. He considers that such poetry as it has inspired is 'mostly very bad indeed'. He finds that 'the most effective piece on Dartmoor is *The Hill Farm*, by Richard John King, written with real feeling and exact description'. I have been unable to locate this book, but discovered that in a little story about a cat abandoned as a kitten on Dartmoor and learning to fend for itself, by G. D.

Griffiths, *Abandoned*,* the great high moor is most vividly described in all its aspects.

George Gissing spent two years in Exeter, from 1890 to 1893, but in a letter to his brother, dated 11 April 1893, wrote that on the whole he feared he had wasted two years in Devon, and that it was obviously in London that his material lay, and by 16 May he had taken 'the upper part of a house in Brixton', though a year later he left London again and moved to Surrey, first to Dorking and then to Epsom, with a summer interlude in Clevedon, Somerset. For a while, however, he liked Exeter, where he had a house 'in the highest part, not a quarter of an hour's walk from the heart of the city, yet within sight of absolute rurality'. He found the surrounding country 'delightful', and walked 'though wonderful hilly lanes to a village called Stoke Canon'. That was in January 1891, but just over two years later he was hankering for London, and the following year was indulging a fantasy of a house in the Mendips, having fallen in love with Wells, with its 'glorious Cathedral', and its wonderful Bishop's Palace, and all of it 'a marvellous spot, civilized with the culture of centuries, yet quite unlike the trimness of other cathedral towns'. But nothing came of that dream, and he took the house at Epsom – from which he could make trips to London. Stoke Canon is four miles from Exeter on the Tiverton main road, and is today a nondescript place, with paper mills, and a church rebuilt in the mid-nineteenth century.

Keats, as we have seen, though he liked the dairymaids, and had moments of liking the rural scenery around Teignmouth, on the whole disliked the Devon scene and the Devon people, and was glad to return to London.

An earlier poet, Robert Herrick, had thirty years of Devon – in two spells – and a curious love–hate relationship with the county as seen from his vicarage at Dean Prior, a village on the south-eastern slopes of Dartmoor. He was presented with the living of Dean Prior in 1629, when he was thirty-eight, by the king, and ejected from it by the Puritans – he was an ardent Royalist – in 1648, one of the numerous dispossessed clergy. He returned to London and published

* Universal-Tandem, a Target book, 1974.

his *Hesperides* poems. He left what he had called 'the loathèd West' with rapturous joy . . . tinged, also, paradoxically, with a shade of regret that since he was 'driven hence' he would no more

> ' . . . *hear a choir*
> *Of merry crickets by my country fire.*'

Yet he had written of the local people as

> '*A people currish, churlish as the seas,*
> *And rude almost as rudest savages*'.

He had declared, also

> '*Search the worlds of ice, and rather there*
> *Dwell than in loathèd Devonshire.*'

When he set out for London, following his dispossession, he vowed that he would never return until

> '*Rocks turn to rivers, rivers turn to men.*'

Nevertheless, fourteen years later he was back, reinstated, and ministered to his parish for another twelve years, until his death at the age of eighty-three in 1674.

When he first took up the living at Dean Prior he felt himself 'banished', cut off from all literary and social life. He found the life of a country parson dull after the lively literary and social life he had led in London, with the poets and wits of the London taverns, where he was a friend of Ben Jonson, and known to his distinguished friends as 'the music of a feast'. Ben Jonson was for him the 'rare arch-poet' and his poetic father. He was also on intimate terms with the musicians of Charles's court and was a courtier poet. Many of his lyrics were written to be set to music and sung before the King in Whitehall, and a number from the *Hesperides* collection were. When he entered holy orders he vowed to give up poetry, and wrote a poem declaring that intention and ending with the word 'Farewell'. But the Muse was not so easily silenced, and in addition to the *Hesperides* lyrics there were the religious poems of *The Noble Numbers*.

He was a poet of mood; he wrote *Discontents in Devon*, but also *His Content in the Country*. In the former he wrote that

> '*More discontents I never had*
> *Since I was born than here,*
> *Where I have been, and still am sad,*
> *In this dull Devonshire.*'

Nevertheless he felt bound to add:

> '*Yet, justly too, I must confess*
> *I ne'er invented such*
> *Ennobled numbers for the press,*
> *Than where I loathed so much.*'

An admission that the Muse was active even in 'dull Devonshire', of the 'loathèd West'.

In the poem on his content in the country he wrote of the peacefulness of his Vicarage life with his faithful housekeeper, Prudence Baldwin:

> '*Here, here I live with what my Board,*
> *Can with the smallest cost afford,*
> *Though ne'er so mean the Viands be,*
> *They well content my Prew and me . . .*
> *Here we rejoice because no Rent*
> *We pay for our poor Tenement;*
> *Wherein we rest and never feare*
> *The Landlord, or the Userer;*
> *The Quarter-day do's ne'er afright*
> *Our Peacefull slumbers in the night.*
> *We eat our own, and batten more,*
> *Because we feed on no man's score . . .*
> *We blesse our Fortunes, when we see*
> *Our own beloved privacie;*
> *And like our living, where w'are known*
> *To very few, or else to none.*'

In a long poem, *A Thanksgiving to God, for his House*, in *Noble Numbers*, he expresses a similar contentment. He wrote, also, numerous poems in praise of country customs and festivals, all maypoles and morris dancing, hay-wains and wassails – together with scurrilous epigrams about some of his parishioners.

As his biographer, F. W. Moorman,* says, it is not easy to

* *Robert Herrick; a biographical and critical study*, 1910.

determine from the conflicting poems 'how far he appreciated his Devonshire home, and how far it seemed to him a place of bitter exile', but he was living through a period of Civil War and, as Moorman points out, 'we do not know with any certainty to what extent the poet's parishioners sympathized with the Puritan party. . . . But we can realize that in Dean Prior, as throughout the country, those years of strife must have sorely tried the better feelings of many an English home. . . . Herrick could not have escaped from all this, and the bitterness of his feelings finds utterance in verse.'

He was remembered in the Dean Prior area, and many of his poems treasured by the parish, long after he had been forgotten in London. Moorman cites an article by Barron Field in the *Quarterly Review* for August 1810, in which the writer records finding many people in the village who could repeat some of his lines, 'and none who were not acquainted with his *Farewell to Dean Bourn*, which, they said, he uttered as he crossed the brook upon being ejected by Cromwell from the vicarage to which he had been presented by Charles I', and they recalled that he saw it again when he was reinstated after the Restoration.

He is buried in an unmarked grave in the little churchyard of his church, St George's, which dates from the fifteenth century, and four years after his death Prudence Baldwin was also buried there, and her grave, too, is unmarked. A tablet to Herrick was set up in the church in 1857, by Perry Herrick, a descendant of a branch of the family, and in the churchyard there is a slab lying on the grass, between two rose-bushes, stating that Robert Herrick was the vicar in this parish 1629–49 and 1662–71, and that he died on 12 October 1674 at the age of eighty-three. At the bottom of the slab there is a quotation from a Herrick lyric: *Gather ye rosebuds while ye may*. The day I was there someone had laid a posy consisting of a primrose, a forget-me-not, and a daisy on the slab.

The churchyard is approached by a lych gate, and there is a big old yew-tree presiding over ancient leaning tombstones, and a near-distance view of the south-eastern slopes of Dartmoor. The church tower has been hideously stuccoed,

but the church itself is of the local granite. The interior is
bare and barnlike, with a raftered roof originally barrelled.
There is an elaborate memorial to Sir Edward Giles, the
lord of the manor in Herrick's time, with an epitaph by
Herrick:

> *'No trust to metals, not to marbles, when*
> *These have their fate and wear away as men.*
> *Time, titles, trophies may be lost and spent,*
> *But virtue rears the eternal monument.*
> *What more than these can tombs or tombstones pay?*
> *But here's the sunset of a tedious day.*
> *These two asleep are; I'll but be undrest*
> *And so to bed. Pray wish us all good rest.'*

The monument is framed by marble pillars and has
kneeling figures of the Giles family.

There is a memorial East Window to Herrick, dedicated
in 1926; in it Herrick is depicted, kneeling, at Dean Court,
the home of Sir Edward Giles, then patron of the living, and
also King Charles I, St George and a Nativity scene. Sir
Edward Giles's coat-of-arms appears at the base of the
window. The whole forms an attractive example of modern
stained glass.

At the entrance to the church, on the tower screen, there
is a charming small copper tablet, by a modern craftsman,
commemorating Prudence Baldwin, and this also has an
epitaph by Herrick:

> *'In this little urn is laid*
> *Prewdence Baldwin (once my maid)*
> *From whose happy spark here let*
> *Spring the purple violet.'*

At the bottom of the tablet there is a small medallion of
coloured glass violets.

For the rest there is a small Norman font, at which Herrick
would have conducted many christenings, and a window
dedicated to his successor, Perry Keene, who was vicar for
fifty years; the window depicts Biblical scenes. It is bright
and attractive like all the glass.

Adjacent to the churchyard is the Old Parsonage, but it is

not Herrick's vicarage but a modern house into which Herrick's parlour, kitchen, and small hall have been incorporated.

When Moorman wrote his biography in 1910 he found Dean Prior a pleasant scattered village with thatched cottages and apple orchards; today it is a nothing of a place, 'a parish without a village' Hoskins calls it, and through which you could drive without noticing it. It is divided by the main Plymouth road, with a non-stop stream of cars and lorries, with the church and parsonage at one side and a farmhouse at the other. Dean Court is a little distance down this motorway, at Lower Dean. It is now a farmhouse and has been largely stuccoed, though a section left untouched, with a small mullioned window, gives an indication of how beautiful a Tudor house it was in the original grey stone. A worn, roughly cobbled yard flanked by stuccoed outhouses was probably the forecourt of the house in Sir Edward Giles's time. Pevsner refers to a Tudor porch and several seventeenth-century windows.

Rose Macaulay wrote a novel centred on Dean Prior in Herrick's time, *They Were Defeated*, first published in 1932.* Herrick figures largely throughout the story, during his first ministry at Dean Prior, and Rose Macauley devotes a Postscript to his leaving when 'outed' in 1647. She wrote that he had 'no great objection' to leaving Dean Prior, and was 'even in a way relieved that his turn had come . . . now that the west was quite lost to the King'. C. V. Wedgwood, in an introduction to the new edition of the novel in 1960, wrote that 'Robert Herrick presides over the book'.

In a charming little book published in 1854, by the Reverend H. J. Whitfield, *Rambles in Devonshire, with Tales and Poetry*, the author described riding to Dean Court on horseback from Totnes, and though he wrote lyrically about the scenery he was at first sight disappointed with the mansion, finding it 'a shadow of a great name, fallen from its high estate, and looking very much like a place in Chancery'. It was by then – 1853 – already 'only a farm house'. But he was interested in the interior, because 'many a time had Herrick and his friend, Sir Edward Giles . . . sat beside that

---

* New edition 1960. Reprinted 1966.

wide hearth, lamenting the evil days, and making perhaps the old rafters ring with the chorus of some Cavalier ditty'. He was severe in his strictures on Herrick for being bored at Dean Prior, but is not fair to him, because he quotes only his poems of Discontent and nothing of his Content. He himself was enraptured with Dean Prior. 'I do not know a valley more lovely than Dean,' he wrote. 'Dartmoor seems to shut it in from the troubles of the world. The querulous reproaches of poor Herrick sound harshly there, and discordantly, out of place.' He concluded his piece by citing a guide book which 'tells us, "The Author of the Hesperides, lived in this place", to which some rustic cicerone adds, "and he didn't like it".'

Writers still gravitate to Devon – and like it. Henry Williamson is, of course, much associated with the county through his books, and now lives in North Devon, at Ilfracombe. Jean Rhys lives in a village near Exeter. The late Eric Delderfield had a large and handsome house in Shaldon, facing the river Teign – I often regarded it with interest and admiration, little dreaming that some years later I would myself live on the slopes above it. Unlike Herrick and Gissing I do not feel exiled here, and do not miss London. Devonshire is not dramatic in the way that Cornwall is; it is perhaps less interesting and stimulating, but it has the vast moor, with its scenic diversity of wild bareness and wooded beauty, and its rocky Tors, which, as the Reverend Whitfield observed, 'dwell grandly apart, with a romance and history of their own'. Not to mention the splendid sunsets on occasion.

All in all, it is the ideal place for reflection – in the Henry Ryecroft manner.

PART III

Sunset Reflections

II

An inquiry into belief in 'God'

The vicar's call set me thinking about this whole question of belief in 'God' on which the three great religions of the world, Christianity, Judaism, and Islam, are founded. Instead of that session of social small talk I should have availed myself of the opportunity to ask a professing and professional Christian to define to me, the unbeliever, what he meant by belief in 'God', what he understood by 'God'. I did not do so because the purely routine visit to the new parishioner did not call for – or induce – any serious conversation. Also, the question, bluntly put, has a certain 'explain-yourself-Sir!' aggressiveness about it. But for a long time after this visit I turned this question over in my mind: what do people who declare that they 'believe in God' *mean* by it, *understand* by it? I decided to try and find out.

I asked various of my friends and acquaintances, including a Muslim and a Jew. I found a general tendency to define 'God' as the Supreme Spirit controlling the universe, the Life Force, the Creator of the universe. Those who defined God in these terms did not put forward any personalized idea of a Being to approach with prayer or worship. They used the term 'God' rather as a convenience term.

But I began with a highly intelligent Catholic priest, who was more concise . . . though in a sense he opted out from the outset by declaring that God, being ineffable, is 'utterly beyond definition or classification'. He went on to cite the Buddha, who, when asked about God, 'maintained a noble silence', adding that he 'could not have done better'. But he also cited Jesus, who said that those who had to give witness to him would be guided by the Holy Spirit what to speak, 'and this one hopes for'. To this he added that many simple people had, he thought, an *awareness* of God while at the same time might be unable to say in any intelligible fashion what they *mean* by God. A favourite modern idea was that God was the *ground* of our being, and of all existence, and the 'supreme spirit controlling the universe', which I had suggested as a possible answer to the question, seemed a good enough answer. He mentioned that 'the scholastics, (Thomas Aquinas *et al*), speak of God as the Necessary Being, the Self-Subsisting Being, the Being who cannot not exist, and who is Pure Being, i.e. with God his *existence* is identical with *his nature*; that is, God's existence is not a *quality* that he possesses and has received. God *is* his own existence; and as such is the *source* of all other existences whatsoever, creating and sustaining them.' He himself, he wrote, thought of God 'basically as the psyche of the universe', adding that the idea was not original to him, and he was not sure where it came from – 'probably either Jung or Ouspensky. I believe it comes from Jung.'

He continued that he thought also of God 'as the supreme eternal Consciousness. What is found in the effect must be present, *in some way*, in the cause. If man is conscious (and self-conscious), "intelligent", etc., then to explain him there must be an eternal consciousness. Nothing can come from nothing. If there were *no* "God", there ought to be *nothing*. Instead we find the "blaze of being (GKC) that we know as the universe".'

He concluded, 'If God is supreme consciousness and supreme *being* ("ens", existence) then he can be both loved and worshipped, even though we now see and know him only as it were through a glass darkly.'

This is a reasoned statement, though it involves metaphysics, and I do not personally subscribe to the idea of man's intelligence and self-consciousness derived from an 'eternal consciousness'. My own thought is along the lines of biological processes, and man's intelligence determined by biological factors.

A Catholic friend wrote me in terms of the creed, believing in God the Father Almighty and his only son Our Lord, and of acceptance of the divine mystery without understanding –

the Catholic precept of 'the faith that precedes reason' which proved an unsurmountable stumbling block for me during my Irish years when I had one foot over the threshold of the Catholic Church.

A Church of England clergyman – not the local vicar – replied on a postcard that God was Jesus . . . to which my reaction was that God existed – in Judaism – long before the advent of Jesus, but I did not debate the issue. I had asked for a definition and been given it; I was not debating anything. It was because of Jesus, he wrote, that he knew something about God.

Dr John Robinson, Bishop of Woolwich, in his controversial little book, *Honest to God*, published in 1963, defines God as 'the ground of our being; a depth at the centre of life'. He devotes an entire chapter to this, citing Tillich and Bonhoeffer, and also Kierkegaard's definition as 'a deeper immersion in existence'. He considers that Love is the ground of our being, and so God is love. All this is highly metaphysical and difficult for the ordinary person, but he makes a cogent point when he writes that 'the necessity for the name "God" lies in the fact that our being has depths which naturalism, whether evolutionary, mechanistic, dialectical or humanistic, cannot or will not recognise'. He cites Tillich on humanity's feeling for the mystery of life and its need for the grip of an 'ultimate meaning of existence', for which naturalism cannot account. For him 'the question of God is the question *whether this depth of being is a reality or an illusion*, not whether a Being exists beyond the bright blue sky, or anywhere else. Belief in God is "what makes you take seriously without reservation", or what for you is ultimate reality.'

I find this unsatisfactory as a definition of 'God'; there are things – causes – which many of us take seriously without any reservation, but they are intellectual convictions plus our sense of justice, and what is true for one person is by no means necessarily true for another; I cannot find that they add up to any belief in God, or have anything to do with it.

I made some inquiries into Quaker belief and found some interesting definitions – 'an indefinable immensity', 'the great scientist', 'the Great Experimenter', 'that power which we can never describe and cannot truly imagine, but which we call God', 'the creator of the material world . . . utterly beyond our understanding', 'the spiritual environment we call God', God as 'the heavenly father', and 'that of God in every man' – this last being a basic Quaker belief, and which I find A. S. Neill expressed in reply to a question about how children should get their first ideas of God; he replied, 'Who is God? I don't know. God to me means the good in each of us.'*

Non-believing friends tried to be helpful. One wrote that for her God was the Life Force, 'the smallest component part of an atom, the ultimate of ultimates, that motivates life in the universe – nothing to be communicated with, but "something" that in rare, ineffable moments, can be tuned into!' She added that Blake's 'God in a grain of sand' was akin to what she was trying to express.

Another friend wrote that he suspected that most people didn't quite know what they mean by 'God' – which is my own view. This friend found 'God' a convenient label 'for a power, a force which I'm sure exists, and which manifests itself in various ways; a power coming to fruition slowly in the immense movements of the human spirit. A power which *underlies* everything, from the construction of an atom or molecule to a symphony by Mozart, and a power with which one can either strive to live in harmony or not. Jesus (and others) seem to have been "in tune with" this power. . . . This is what I *understand* by what I mean by the label "God". I don't know much about *Belief*. . . . I must be able to see some "reality", however dimly.'

A Church of England friend wrote that her idea of God was of a Supreme Spirit; that she got a sense of 'peace and calm' from going to Church, and particularly from taking Holy Communion. She believes in prayer – though how you make the personal approach of prayer, which is supplication, to a *spirit* no one has attempted to explain to me. For a time in young womanhood this friend was an atheist, believing that 'commonsense ruled out God'. She married a believing Muslim and reverted to belief in God. She believes in astrology and in reincarnation. She finds the ritual of the Church 'comforting and warm', liking the priestly robes and the music, and the beauty of churches, and considers

* Summerhill: a radical approach to child-rearing, 1960.

that these things are 'acceptable in the worship of God'.

Her Muslim husband wrote me at some length on his 'belief in the presence of God.' God for him is the 'invisible power behind the universe', designing human life from birth to death. He is a fatalist, citing the Islamic *Mektoub*, 'it is written'. He set forth his Islamic beliefs, but these were not new to me, and anyhow outside the scope of my inquiry.

An Islamic scholar, a Jewish convert to Islam, and a translator of the Qur'ān, wrote to me that it is 'a fundamental axiom of Islam that God is *undefinable* since He is not comparable to anyone or anything else, as well as outside all limitations of time and space. All terms applied to God are merely circumscriptions of the perceptible *effects* of His activity and cannot have the character of a definition.' He referred me to the Qur'ān, to the Sixth Sūrah, Al-An'ām ('Cattle'), verse 100 – 'Limitless is He in His glory, and sublimely exalted above anything that man may devise by way of definition: the originator of the heavens and the earth.' The footnote to the reference to 'definition' yields more for my purpose: 'The very concept of "definition" implies the possibility, of a comparison or correlation of an object with other objects; God, however, is unique, there being "nothing like unto Him" and, therefore, "nothing that could be compared with Him" – with the result that any attempt at defining Him or His "attributes" is a logical impossibility, and, from the ethical point of view, a sin. The fact that He is indefinable makes it clear that the "attributes" (*sifāt*) of God mentioned in the Qur'ān do not circumscribe His reality but, rather, the perceptible *effect of his activity* on and within the universe created by Him.'

The Sūrah continues: 'No human vision can encompass him, whereas He encompasses all human vision; for He alone is unfathomable, all-aware.'

So far as I am concerned this is a definition, albeit to my materialist mind incomprehensible.

For the Jewish definition I wrote to an American rabbi I knew – only to discover that he was not orthodox, but in the Reform tradition, and this being so, he wrote, his beliefs might not fit in with my inquiries, but 'on the chance that they might be of some interest' he would set them down. He had never, he wrote, consciously thought about God-definitions, and there was a caveat, he thought, in Maimonides, against speculating too much about the character of God – 'it is, as I recall the caution, like looking too long at the sun. It can blind the viewer.' Furthermore, 'Judaism is a religion notable for avoiding dogma. And since, to be candid, we know so little about God what those more certain than I "know" must be mostly dogmatics.'

His belief in God, he wrote, was in many ways comprised of negatives – he was more certain what *not* to believe. He was, he supposed, an 'inner-directed' person. By a process of deduction he had concluded that he did believe in God, but for him any God-definition was a highly personal, intimate matter. He seriously doubted that there was any super-man, any super-power *physical* force, ordering the stars in their ways or causing any specific sparrow to fall. 'Probably science,' he wrote, 'with all of its still unresolved shortcomings, either has provided us with more rational explanations for the universe and its way; or may still do so. In any event, I am not satisfied with a God who **is** only what is left over after science runs out of answers at some moment in history.'

That is a statement which speaks very much to my own condition, but I do not 'go along', as the Americans say, with his final summing-up: 'But when all the negatives are sifted out I find I still believe there is a certain immutability and inexorability to some moral order. I do not know who – or what – prescribed it. Perhaps it is no more than the cumulative – sometimes almost mindless – experience of history. But virtue, I believe, is rewarded. The reward is not always conferred ostentatiously upon the virtuous individual personally. But like the physical laws of energy, I believe virtue is never lost and somehow – despite the advertising industry's proclivities for the quick cure – it is added to the cumulative wisdom and experience of human kind. And, *vice-versa* with "sin". In this sense of judging the worth of "virtue" and the waste of "sin" I think "God's time" is not always – is rarely – the same as our own.' All this, he stresses, is his own personal view; for the orthodox answer I must consult 'any standard Jewish theological work'.

I am thrown back on a Quaker assertion – in a discussion of Quaker belief* – that God is not to be imagined or given any form or shape – 'any attempt to do this can only make it less real [to us] and any stand in the way of experience . . . we do not *believe* in this divine; we *know it* from experience'. That experience 'we may call God; but some dare not even give it a title let alone a name. It is quite incredible and therefore beyond belief. Only experience, which is open to all, can manifest it.' Another contributor to the discussion pointed out that 'the word, "God" can mean to a Teilhard de Chardin, "the creator of all that is"; but to a child the word could mean "Gentle Jesus meek and mild".' This writer spoke of 'creeds' or 'firm beliefs' as 'mere verbalizations' which could be 'disruptive', the strength of Jesus being that he brought us back to the realization that 'the true God is the creator'.

From the journal of the Society of Friends I turned to that of the Rationalist Press Association, *The New Humanist*, and in their issue of December 1974 found that in a poll carried out by the Opinion Research Centre, under the sponsorship of the B.B.C., only 29 per cent of the population believe in a personal God, compared with 38 per cent of professed belief in 1963. 35 per cent believed in a Creative Spirit or Life Force, which is 2 per cent more than in 1963. 6 per cent were atheist, not believing in any form of God, comparing with 9 per cent in 1963. The remaining 39 per cent were don't knows. Hector Hawton, acting editor of *The New Humanist*, commenting on this 'poll on God', says that 'these findings should be scrutinized with care, much depends on the adjective "personal". I doubt whether it applies to the God of Voltaire or Thomas Paine. It clearly does not apply to the Unmoved Mover of Aristotle who was merged by Christian theologians with the dynamic and quite unspeakable tribal Yahweh' – Jehovah. Hawton goes on to say that he is often asked whether a Humanist can believe in God, and he would reply to that with a further question: 'Were Paine and Voltaire, not to mention Spinoza and Einstein, Humanists? I should hesitate to excommunicate anyone who believed – to use Pascal's classification – in the God of the Philosophers,'

* *The Friend*, 21 February, 1975.

he goes on, but concludes, 'But no Humanist, certainly no Rationalist, can believe in the God of Abraham, Isaac and Jacob.'

In the February 1975 issue of *The New Humanist* I found an article by Fenner Brockway on *Socialism as Humanism*, in the course of which he declared himself an agnostic – 'I don't know whether there is a God', adding that there were experiences which prevented him from being dogmatic. If there is a Creative Force, he says, he doesn't know, being an agnostic, whether that implies a God, 'but it certainly does not imply an intervening personal God'. I feel that the key word there is 'intervening' – implying a personally approachable God, to be worshipped, and supplicated by prayer, a God with the human attributes of love and mercy. Brockway cites an opinion poll showing that 53 per cent of people never went to church, and compares it with over a third of the people consulted believing in some Creative Life Force, as opposed to a Personal God, which, as he says, shows 'how unrepresentative is allegiance to the Churches'.

St Augustine of Hippo had a highly personal conception of a Personal God. The whole of his *Confessions* is addressed to this Personal God – 'Late have I loved Thee, Beauty so ancient and so new! Late have I loved Thee!'* Seeking a definition of God he put his question to the earth – to the sea and sky and winds, the moon and stars, and all things created, and 'clear and loud they answered, "God is he who made us." '† But he found that God was even more – that 'He is the Life of the life of my soul'. St Augustine of Hippo was the complete, unequivocal – the *impassioned* – believer, and even so late in the day, with my own belief totally negated, I find reading his *Confessions* a moving experience.

I was interested in an article in *The Times*, 27 January 1975, by the Chief Rabbi, in which he urged that religion alone could lead civilization away from the brink of disaster. 'There can be no brotherhood of Man without the Fatherhood of God,' he declared, adding that it was 'only as children of a common God that we humans are brothers. Take away the link and the chain of human fraternity and

* F. J. Sheed's translation.
† R. S. Pine-Coffin's translation.

understanding disintegrates.' I found this an astonishing statement – but not peculiar to Judaism. The Christians also postulate no brotherhood of Man without the Fatherhood of God. I was interested that Nicolas Walter, the managing editor of the Rationalist Press Association, replied to this article in a letter to *The Times* dated 1 February 1975. He wrote that contrary to the Chief Rabbi's suggestion he would suggest that 'we are biological rather than theological brothers, linked by being one species rather than by being creatures of one God, and much more likely to avoid disaster if we apply reason to our actual human situation than if we rely on faith in an assumed divine providence'. He concluded, cogently, 'The record of religious leaders in the history of the past few thousand years hardly suggests that they will be much use in the future. If mankind is saved, it will be by the commonsense of rational individuals, not by the dogmatism of appointed authority.' To which I, personally, would say Amen.

But the inquiry interested me as manifesting a general human desire for some sort of conception of God – the need to explain the universe, and to believe in 'Something'.

In 1940, between January and September, in Connemara, I worked on a book about religion, which I called *Christianity – or Chaos*, with the sub-title, *A Re-statement of Religion*. Amongst the very simple Catholic country people of the West of Ireland I found that a very personal conception of God was, as they said there, 'nearer than the door', and the turf smoke, and the Catholicism, of what I called 'the spirit of Ireland', blows across the pages of the book, but looking at it again, some thirty-five years later, I found it in general valid. In an introductory chapter I wrote of 'The Search for "God"' and that 'men and women necessarily find "God", as they find Love and Beauty, in divers ways. For some "God" is reached through the intercession of the Blessed Virgin, before candle-lit altars and shrines. For others "God" breathes in the austere atmosphere of a Quaker meeting-house, bare as a ship and full of quietness and meditation. Others, again, find "God" in the pagan manner, through communion with nature, and the spontaneous animal impulses of physical energy and procreativeness as sacraments and thanksgiving for the gift of life. Some would seem to attempt to evolve a personal Deity who is a cross between Jehovah and Jesus. For some God is Allah; for others a more generalized Supreme Being.'

When I wrote that I had, as I have said, one foot over the threshold of the Church of Rome; I did not get the other foot over because the more I thought and read, and discussed with priests, the more I found myself incapable of the necessary suspension of disbelief. After that, when I returned from Burma, in the 'fifties, I read a good deal about Thereveda Buddhism, in the pursuit of 'religion without God', but even Buddhism involved some belief in the supernatural – and of that I was, and remain, incapable. I want a scientific explanation for everything . . . even for 'God', which, I fully realize, is a contradiction in terms.

Freud dismissed religious belief as obsolete illusion, and a neurosis. Bertrand Russell, in his essay on Free Thought in his *Sceptical Essays*,* declared himself a dissenter from all known religions and expressed the hope that religious belief would die out. 'I do not believe,' he wrote, 'that, on the balance, religious belief has been a force for good. Although I am prepared to admit that in certain times and places it has had some good effects, I regard it as belonging to the infancy of human reason, and to a stage of development we are now outgrowing.' That was written over fifty years ago, and it expresses the views I personally held then and hold today. It is interesting that in 1975 an Opinion Poll found that only 21 per cent of the people questioned – representative of all sections of the community – went to church more than once a month, and 53 per cent never. But as against that we have 64 per cent believing in either a Personal God or a Creative Spirit or Life-Force, as against only 6 per cent who were flat-out Atheists and 39 per cent Don't Know. There is obviously a reluctance – and I found it in my own inquiry – to admit to complete atheism, total disbelief in any form of 'God'; atheist has a harsh sound – 'as harsh as truth' – and 'agnostic' is a comfortable compromise, leaving the door open to doubt and possibility alike; it is a gentle word. The only out-and-out atheist I came across in

*1922.

my inquiry was a young anarchist friend – a man in his mid-thirties – and he made no bones about it, though his wife prefers to call herself an agnostic.

In an evaluation of the films of Ingmar Bergman,* Roger Manvell says that in his introduction to his film, *Wild Strawberries*, Bergman – who had a strict Lutheran up-bringing – writes: 'To me, religious problems are continuously alive. I never cease to concern myself with them. . . . Yet this does not take place on the emotional level, but on an intellectual one. Religious emotion, religious sentimentality is something I got rid of long ago – I hope. The religious problem is an intellectual one to me: the relation of my mind to my intuition.'

Manvell also quotes Peter Cowie in *Sweden*, 'one of Tantivy Press film series', as saying: 'Bergman is apparently fond of quoting Eugene O'Neill's claim that all dramatic art is worthless unless it deals with man's relationship to God. For Bergman, there has to be some power in the universe (he calls it God for want of a better word), a power that influences man's mind and situation. He is interested in this God because he feels him, more than social and economic conditions, to be responsible for all the complexes, vanities, and desires that man is heir to, and which reduce him to a posturing idiot.'

I am a great admirer of Eugene O'Neill as a dramatist, but I cannot find that his plays deal with man's relationship to God; nor can I see that Bergman's television series, *Six Scenes from a Marriage*, has anything to do with that relationship – unless sex is an aspect of God. Perhaps as an expression of the Life Force it is.

In all these inquiries I drew only one blank, and that was from a High Anglican priest who after keeping me waiting two months for a reply – by which time the stamp on the s.a.e. I had enclosed had become out-of-date – wrote that as I was what he called 'not a Theist' anything he could say would be of no use – though what my atheism had to do with his Theism I do not understand, and it was a definition of his Theism I sought. I wrote thanking him for his 'very inter-

* In *The New Humanist*, December, 1974.

esting' letter, and certainly that a professional Christian should refuse to co-operate with a non-believer who was merely seeking information – enlightenment, if you like – is extremely interesting.

It was all, anyhow, a very interesting piece of research though in fact I need have gone no further than the *Oxford Dictionary* for the definition of 'God': 'Superhuman worshipped as having power over human nature and fortunes; deity ... Supreme Being, Creator and Ruler of the universe', and going on to God with a capital G as the 'Lord God, Almighty God; God of the Father, Son, Holy Ghost'. But I had wanted to find out what ordinary people, as well as priests, believed by, understood by, their profession of belief in God, and for the most part of it seems to be – as the Opinion Pool cited – a vague belief in some kind of Supreme Spirit behind the universe and all life, and to a lesser degree a personalized God to be approached by prayer and worship. Belief in some such Life Force or Supreme Spirit conveniently explains the universe and exonerates the believer from the harsh charge of atheism, but such beliefs are what my rabbi friend calls 'the answers left over from science'. Belief in God is personalized as the Heavenly Father, of infinite love and mercy, is a kind of insurance policy against the stresses of life, because, if you can really believe it, behind all calamity and all sorrow there is this infinite compassion. For many there has to be God and Heaven to make life on this earth bearable, with the compensation of the hope of a happier life hereafter.

This belief in a personal God must be immensely comforting, but how earthquakes and cyclones, floods and famines, not to mention cancer – inflicted even on children, even on animals – how all such evil is to be explained away in terms of a compassionate and all-loving ruler of the universe I shall never understand. Or how God in terms of Divine Spirit can be approached by the prayers of suffering humanity.

For myself I am content to settle for the scientific explanations, however inadequate, and the hope that as scientific knowledge expands Science will come up with more and more of the answers. Until then I will get along as best I can with rationalism, which, so far as I can see, works – pragmatically – quite as well as religious belief. Not only have I no hope of any life hereafter but devoutly hope there is none. One life is *quite* enough. I shall be extremely put out if after my death I wake up in Eternity and find I have to go on, in some form or other, all over again.

As far back as 1941 Julian Huxley wrote, in his *Religion Without Revelation*, that it would 'soon be as impossible for an intelligent, educated man or woman to believe in a god as to believe that the earth is flat'. Nevertheless by the late nineteen-seventies belief in 'God' in some form or other persists for a very great many people – even when they do not attend church, mosque or synagogue. It is significant that in all my inquiries I found only one out-and-out atheist.

"the god of the gaps"

A reflection on some misused terms

Does a word or a term cease to be misused when 'common usage' sanctions it? For example, in the terms of the dictionary definition the word *nice* is the most abused in our language. The extent to which it has been debased by colloquialism is *a nice point*, but we talk about a nice day, a nice person, a nice dress, a nice place, meaning pleasant, attractive, agreeable. Or we use the word as an adverb and refer to travelling 'nice and fast', or hope the weather will be 'nice and fine' – establishing colloquialisms which, says Fowler, in *Modern English Usage*, 'should be confined, in print, to dialogue'. He goes on to point out that '*nice* has been spoilt, like *clever*, by its *bonnes fortunes*; it has been too great a favourite with the ladies, who have charmed out of it all its individuality and converted it into a mere diffuser of vague and mild agreeableness. Everyone who uses it in its proper senses, which fill most of the space given to it in any dictionary, and avoids the modern one that tends to oust them all, does a real if small service to the language.'

The *Oxford Dictionary* devotes a good deal of space to its meaning, and gives as examples of its correct usage: must not be too nice about the means; a nice experiment, point, question, negotiation; a nice distinction, shade of meaning; a nice ear, judgement, hand; but it allows its colloquial use in nice-looking, meaning of engaging appearance, or of a house standing nice and high . . . accepts, that is to say, its misuse in common usage.

I myself have often observed that it's 'a nice day', or that so-and-so is 'nice', or that that's a nice dress you're wearing, though I am well aware of the misuse of the word, but when it comes to the mis-use of the word *shambles* I draw the line. Yet it is a word commonly used, and particularly by politicians. If we enter/don't enter the E.E.C. the country will be reduced to a shambles, they proclaim. A shambles is a slaughter-house, or a 'place of carnage', and nothing but that. It does not do even as a metaphor, for England will not be running with blood if we enter/do not enter the E.E.C. But redecorating a house the owner will declare that for the duration the place is a shambles, or an office is described as a shambles because the mail has piled up and the wastepaper baskets have not been emptied over a bank holiday weekend. 'Oh, my dear, you should have seen – the place was a *shambles*!' Well, with not a drop of blood anywhere it wasn't. Not by any stretch of imagination or metaphor.

Two other great favourites with politicians and journalists are 'at this moment of time', and 'in this day and age'. The moment can only be of time, and it dissolves as soon as uttered anyhow; what the user means is at the present time, the present point of history; which is what is meant by 'this day and age'; this day can only be of this age.

We talk of a disturbing experience as being 'traumatic', when in fact trauma relates only to the morbid condition of the body produced by a wound or external violence. 'You are bound to find moving a house a traumatic experience,' people constantly assured me. The word is too essentially related to medicine to serve even as hyperbole, or as metaphor for wounds of the spirit. Anyone who has suffered from shock is said to have experienced trauma. It has become a modern catch-phrase, and in the sense in which it is used is meaningless. Like the extraordinary habit of prefacing an anecdote with 'There was this woman' – or man or girl – at the bus stop, at a party or wherever, when all that is meant is 'there was a – ' Perhaps it is an American importation, like the use of the word 'contact' for 'get in touch with', and 'meet with', or 'meet up with' instead of simply meet.

'Basically' is not so much misused as grossly overworked; fundamentally would be the better word, but we do not want too many fundamentals either, since the use is frequently an exaggeration. 'Basically the issue is this,' declare the politicians, when in fact there is nothing which could be correctly described as basic or fundamental about the issue at all.

'Delicious,' also, is commonly used, when the better word would be delightful, since, strictly, delicious applies to taste, smell, and sense of humour. Thus a pudding can be delicious but not a view.

'Field day' is another of them. A field day is a military manoeuvre, but school-children are regularly taken on country outings, for nature study or geological observation, called 'field days'. And a woman who has had a bout of spring-cleaning will declare that she has had a 'field day' – though as metaphor this will perhaps pass.

What will not pass, however, is the commonly accepted misuse of the term 'anti-Semitism' as denoting anti-Jewish-ness. Not all Jews are of Semitic origin, whereas all Arabs are. An anti-Semitic person, therefore, would hate all Arabs and some Jews. Strictly the term Semitic applies to *a group of languages*, or which Arabic and Hebrew are two. The *Oxford Dictionary* defines Semite as a member of any of the races supposed to descend from Shem (*Gen*. x, 21 fol.) including especially the Hebrews, Arameans, Phoenicians, Arabs, and Assyrians. The *Encyclopaedia Britannica* has a long article on the Semitic or Shemitic languages, spoken by the descendants of Shem, and 'spoken in Arabia, Mesopotamia, Syria and Palestine, whence they spread into Egypt, Abyssinia, northern Africa and elsewhere'. A writer to *The Times*, Chester Erskine (21 December 1974), corrected a correspondent who declared that the Arabs were more 'purely Semitic' than the Jews. She was, he thought, under the mistaken notion, which was a common mistaken notion, 'that the Semites are a race of people belonging to the Semitic language group, of which Hebrew is and had always been one', in the same manner that an English person is 'a member of the Indo-European language group and particularly of the Germanic branch of that division, and not a member of the Indo-European race. Further,' he added, 'the Jews in spite of popular misconception are not a race but an aggregate of many races (see *Encylopaedia Britannica*) as

Top Dartington Hall

Above In the grounds at Dartington Hall, the Henry Moore 'Reclining Woman'

Richard II's white hart; the centre boss of the vaulted entrance porch to the Great Hall, Dartington

anthropologists have established. What the Jews are is a religious culture, and one which has spawned both Christian and Muslim religious cultures.' He summed up, 'To be accurate, then, people who choose to hate Jews should be referred to as anti-Jewish, and people who hate Arabs as anti-Arab, and neither as anti-Semitic.'

The interested reader is referred to a valuable work by Dr Ashley Montagu, himself a Jew, *Man's Most Dangerous Myth; the Fallacy of Race*.* He debates the whole fallacy of dividing human beings into races, and disputes that the Jews are even, mentally or physically, an ethnic group, let alone a race. Similarly, in an article in *Issues*,† published by the American Council for Judaism, '*Jewish*' *Biological Race Myth Exploded*, or Marcus Goldstein, reviewing *The Jewish People; a Biological History*,‡ by Harry L. Shapiro, states emphatically that 'there is no Jewish "biological race" ', and quotes from the author on the subject of race generally: 'Although a Churchill, for example, may with great effect speak of the "English race" where "English people" would not do for literary reasons, too many writers, and, alas, too many readers do not clearly differentiate the biological and the literary usage. We encounter, therefore, constant references to the French, Italian, or Spanish race, to the Semitic or Aryan race, to the Anglo-Saxon race, as though attributes of nationality, language or culture were primary criteria of racial distinction. None of these actually has any value in differentiating mankind into biological groups, since they are acquired by residence or learning and are not directly the consequence of genetic processes. The zoological concept of race is founded, on the contrary, primarily on the physical inheritance of anatomical or physiological characteristics. Acquired traits are not permissible. . . .'

If acquired fallacious notions of race lead us to regard people born and bred in the Judaic faith as a race and we choose, irrationally, to dislike them collectively, let us use the correct term and proclaim ourselves, in all the brutality and

* Published by the World Publishing Co., New York, 1965.
† Winter, 1961.
‡ United Nations Educational, Scientific and Cultural Organization, Paris, 1960.

D

stupidity of the term, anti-Jewish; let us not use a high-sounding phase which has no real meaning. In terms of common misusage we could say that it is not *nice*; that it makes a *shambles* of the language, and gives the deluded tribe of racialists a *field day*.

13

Some reflections on Palestine

The misused term 'anti-Semitic' is commonly applied to defenders of the Palestinian cause . . . which is a contradiction in terms, since the Palestinian Arabs are Semites, a fact which wearily, down through the years, I point out to people who charge me with 'anti-Semitism'. I know that by 'anti-Semitic' is meant anti-Jewish, and I explain that I am not anti *people* at all; like most people I like and dislike people because of their personalities – nothing to do with their racial origins, ethnic groupings, religion, or even their ideas. I even like some people whilst intensely disliking some of their ideas. I have liked many Jews and disliked many Arabs. I am neither 'pro-Arab' nor 'anti-Jew'. What I am 'pro' is justice; what I am 'anti' is injustice. I am therefore with the Palestinians in their struggle – which dates from the thirties – for a national identity and to regain their country, Palestine; and I am against Zionism, which robs the Palestinians of their identity and colonizes their country, imposing the racialist, Zionist state of 'Israel' on an ancient Arab land, and in the process displacing and dispossessing over a million Palestinians, an entire nation, who either rot out their lives in camps throughout the Middle East or exist in diaspora throughout the world – exiled and stateless. Mercifully not all Jews are Zionists by any means, and certainly not all Zionists are Jews.

In my experience and observation the majority of the non-Jewish Zionists are ignorant of the basic, historic facts. I am thinking, here, of the average well-meaning, uninformed person who thinks 'Israel' a fine idea, a home for 'the Jews', ignorant of the fact that Jews no more than

Christians or Muslims or Buddhists are a race, or even an ethnic group, and that very many Jews, the world over, do not in the very least identify themselves with the Zionist state – for the simple reason that we inherit our religions, and whether we practise them or not our identity is national, not religious, and people of the Jewish faith are no exception to the rule. Orthodox Jews tend to be less Zionistic than the unorthodox, feeling that Zionism is in opposition to Judaism, which embraces Jews of all nationalities, so that there is no allegiance to 'Israel'. It is interesting – and significant – that many Russian Jews, once they have secured visas to leave the U.S.S.R., for Israel opt for the U.S.A. once they are free, and Israeli officials have been sent to Vienna to persuade Russian Jews to settle in Palestine instead of in Western countries. The Associated Press news agency, reporting on 16 February 1975, stated: 'Western sources in the Soviet Union have been reported as saying that the number of Russian Jewish immigrants that chose to live outside Israel is about forty per cent. Many prefer the United States or European countries, claiming that life in Israel is too dangerous and difficult.' Eric Silver, in *The Guardian*, 10 January, said that about 17 per cent of Soviet Jews failed to continue on to Israel in 1974 compared to 4 per cent in 1973. In fact, during 1974, the proportion rose steadily month by month reaching 20 per cent in August and 35 per cent in December. The report cited Mr Samuel Alder, special adviser to the Minister of Absorption, as stating: 'The most important reason is the snowball effect. More and more Jews realized they could get out of the Soviet Union. So many with no real Jewish motivation began applying. These people never felt that Israel was their spiritual homeland.'

Chaim Bermant, writing in *The Observer*, 15 December 1974, stated cogently, 'What the events of the past four or five years have shown is that there is not so much an irrepressible Jewish yearning for Zion as for freedom and if there is a primary stream of Russian Jews for whom Israel is the fulfilment of a dream, there is a secondary stream for whom it is a gateway to liberty. What we are now witnessing is the growth of a tertiary stream.'

It is significant, too, that during the Nazi persecution many Jews who managed to get out of Germany and Austria wanted to emigrate to America, but the world Zionist organization would only assist them to go to Palestine.

What many well-meaning supporters of 'Israel' do not realize is that when Palestine was partitioned, by the voting at the U.N. in November 1947, for the creation of the Zionist state, two-thirds of the country was given to a third of the population, the Jews, who were not even the Palestinian Jews, for the most part, but foreign immigrants from all over the world – Russians, Poles, Germans, British – with not even a common language, with nothing in common but their religion, which by no means all of them practised. The Balfour Declaration promised – 'viewed with favour' – a Jewish national home in Palestine, not a state. Palestine was to be a Jewish refuge, not a Zionist colony. The Balfour Declaration even postulated the rights of the endemic people of Palestine, the Palestinian Arabs – 'it being clearly understood that nothing shall be done which may prejudice the civil and religious rights of existing non-Jewish communities in Palestine' . . . which were incidentally the majority of the population. (There were about 50,000 Jews in Palestine at that time, and some 670,000 Arabs, Muslim and Christian. The Zionist aspiration was so to intensify Jewish immigration into Palestine that the Jews became a majority, which is the situation today.)

It is possible, indeed it is most probable, that most people who think 'Israel' a good idea do not know these facts – have probably never even heard of the Balfour Declaration. Though since June 1967, when in the six-day war the Palestinians lost still more of their land to the Zionist state, the wind of change began blowing for Palestine; in the so-called Yom Kippur war a few years later the wind blew more strongly still, restoring dignity to the Arab world at large and still further emphasizing the Palestinian national identity. Since then we have had the Rabat Conference in 1974, at which the decision was taken by the Arab leaders to recognize the right of the Palestine Liberation Organization to set up an independent state in any part of Palestine from which Israel withdraws and to define the national rights of the Palestinians: then soon after this the P.L.O. leader, Yasir Arafat, addressed the United Nations Assembly, stating the Palestine case and speaking as the sole representative of the Palestinian people, and received a standing ovation. That King Hussein should ever give up his claim to the West Bank of the Jordan seemed always utterly unlikely, but so strongly did the wind of change blow that the impossible happened.

That the setting up of a Palestinian state can be seriously considered by the outside world is an important part of the wind of change that has swept the Palestinians scene since the 1967 war. Now when the London representative of the P.L.O. puts forward the idea in a paper published by the *Middle East Digest* and debated at a seminar of the Council for the Advancement of Anglo-Arab Understanding, *The Times* (18 March 1975) devotes a whole column to it. And on 20 March 1975, *The Times* runs an eight-page Special Report on the Arab League countries, with an article on the front page by Edward Mortimer, their distinguished Middle East correspondent, headed: As a group Palestinians play an important economic and cultural role. The whole report, by E. C. Hodgkin, Foreign Editor of *The Times*, is entitled *Arab Renaissance*. In his article Edward Mortimer points out that 'the non-existence of Palestine as a state has been, ever since 1948, a key factor in Arab politics. In the Arabs' own eyes it constitutes their greatest defeat and shame. But precisely this shame and the determination to expunge it have been perhaps the greatest unifying factor in the Arab world during the last generation. And the Palestinians themselves, by the very fact of being driven out of their own country, have spread throughout the Arab world like leaven in the dough.' He goes on, later in the article, to say that 'The Palestine Liberation Organization was set up in 1965 as a kind of *ersatz* Palestinian state. It is a full member of the League of Arab States, and its chairman (since 1968 Mr Yassir Arafat) is treated with all the honours of a head of state.' Sir John Richmond contributes a valuable article on The Political Viability of a Palestine State, with full regard for all the difficulties involved, but postulating its possibility given the co-operation of both Israel and the mainstream of

Teddy!

the Palestine movement, together with the support of the Arab League and the sponsorship of the United Nations and the Super Powers.

Before 1967 the possibility that Arafat would ever address the United Nations was as remote as that King Hussein would ever consider conceding the West Bank to the Palestinians in the event of the Israelis relinquishing their Occupied Territory. Before the physical Arab defeat of the June war was turned into a moral victory the P.L.O. was, in the eyes of the world, just a gang of outlawed guerillas, and the Palestinians merely a rabble of 'refugees' festering in camps or scattered in exile throughout the world. Mrs Meier could make her astonishing assertion that there *were* no Palestinians without making herself a laughing stock. Before 1967 you could count on the fingers of one hand the voices raised in England on behalf of the Palestinian cause. The wind of change since then has blown very powerfully for that cause.

In 1973 Mrs Margaret Arakie's short, concise, factual book, *The Broken Sword of Justice: America, Israel and the Palestine Tragedy*, was published.* That this uncompromising book could be published in England simultaneously in hard cover and paperback, and objectively reviewed as the serious analysis that it is, is yet another indication of how strongly the wind has blown in the Palestine direction in the last few years, and how strongly it continues to blow. In her concluding chapter Mrs Arakie writes: '"Palestinian" is no longer synonymous with "refugee"', and points out that the Palestinian resistance movement has become the most dynamic in the Middle East.

Mrs Arakie also draws attention to the hopeful and encouraging 'growing recognition in Israel itself, and not only amongst the young and the "New Left", that the Palestine Arabs were wronged when the Zionist state was created'. This is a wind of change that many of us have been aware of, thankfully, for some time. We have heard voices raised in the Zionist state for the defence of Palestinian rights, and we have seen young men refuse to be conscripted

* Mrs. Arakie was assistant, in the sixties, to Dr. John Davies, the Director General of U.N.W.R.A. in Beirut.

Oh dear! By 2014, deplorable change of wind — tragic, catastrophic

into what they rightly see as an Army of Occupation – it has been freely reported in the British press by reputable journalists. I have myself long contended that the Palestine issue could well be resolved from within Israel itself, because of a generation growing up that begins to ask questions: 'Who *are* we? Who are these Arabs? What *is* this "Israel"? How did it come about?' – and which will grow more and more to understand the development of Zionism in the creation of this colonialist and racialist state imposed on the Palestinians, and to realize that Palestine is endemically Arab, its indigenous people for the last two thousand years the Palestinians.

The importance of this wind of change in Israel itself cannot be over-estimated, even if at present it is no more than a light, surface-ruffling breeze. But this wind is very marked in England, judging by letters to responsible newspapers such as *The Times, The Guardian, The Observer, The Sunday Times*, by the tone of editorials on such issue as the Rabat Conference and the presentation of the Palestine case at the United Nations, by the publication by *The Times* of the Arab Special Report, by informed articles, sympathetic to the Palestinian point of view, and also in general conversation with all kinds of people.

Before 1967 much was heard about Israel and its achievements, and almost nothing about the Palestinians and their aspirations. After the June war the issue was discussed as freely as other major world issues, and without the emphasis always being on 'gallant little Israel menaced on all sides by Arab hordes'. It is not too much to say now, I think, that there is a considerable pro-Palestinian minority of public opinion in England, surviving even the tragic – and damaging – acts of Palestinian terrorists such as the hi-jackings of 'planes and the holding of hostages in embassies. Public feeling is strong about such criminally stupid acts, but, in my observation, the people who believe that the Palestinians have a case do not withdraw their convictions and sympathies because of them. They deplore them, but the basic justice of the case remains, along with the basic injustice which provokes such mistaken acts. That the majority of public opinion is still sympathetic in the main to the Israelis is probably true, and appears to be based largely on the fallacious idea of the Biblical right of Jews to the Promised Land, but there is this swing of sympathy and understanding towards the Palestinians, particularly since the victorious October war of 1973 and Arafat's success at the United Nations.

This wind of change is something which we Palestine 'Old Hands' did not expect to live to see, but we cannot fail to be aware of it, and it is for the Palestinians themselves to take intelligent, constructive advantage of it, until it sweeps even that vast stronghold of Zionism, the U.S.A., without whose economic aid the Zionist state could not exist.

Such hopes!   2014-'15
Everyone being so stupid.
Eg. the Islamist Jihadis in Europe who, if
their concern was really for Palestinians,
would not be trying to frighten all Jews
into migrating to Israel, where they would
surely "need" to be rehomed on yet
more farm land stolen from Palestinians

14

The time of my life

Some years ago there was a radio series in which well-known people were interviewed about what he or she considered 'the time of my life'. I was not invited to contribute to the series, but if I had been I should not have said that the time of my life was when I was young and gay, and a successful journalist and rising young writer, in the 'twenties, but the early years of the 'sixties, when I was to-ing and fro-ing between London and the Middle East as the guest of the various Arab governments, collecting material for books, doing something that intensely interested me, and feeling myself useful – serving a cause in which I passionately believed. I had, then, a sense of fulfilment I had never had before and have never had since.

My first journey to the Middle East was in January 1962 when I flew to Baghdad as the guest of General Qassim's government, after which I visited Jordan, the Lebanon, Syria, Egypt, including the Gaza Strip, then administered by Egypt, and wrote *A Lance for the Arabs*, published at the beginning of 1963. I travelled widely in Iraq and met General Qassim; was invited as a government guest to Kuwait and went, but did not at that time write about it, my allegiance being to Qassim's Iraq and there was tension between the two countries at that time. In Jordan I stayed first with a Jordanian doctor and his Irish wife in Amman, and then in Jericho with the distinguished Palestinian, Musa Alami, on his famous desert-reclamation farm and agricultural project. In Beirut I was the guest of that remarkable Lebanese, the millionaire, Emile Bustani. In

Damascus I was the guest of the Ministry of Foreign Affairs, and in Cairo of the Ministry of Information, under whose auspices I was duly taken to Gaza. I saw my first Palestine refugee camp outside Jericho, and later was to visit even more terrible ones outside Beirut and Damascus. Of all this I wrote in *A Lance for the Arabs*, which was designed as a travel book which would also state the Palestine case and speak for the displaced and dispossessed Palestinians, loosely referred to as 'refugees'. I dedicated the book to them.

It was in Gaza, on that first occasion, that I looked along the road to Beersheba, the ancient Palestinian town then – as now – part of the Zionist state; and there, also, that I saw a dead shepherd, killed by an Israeli bullet, brought back across the border, and, profoundly moved – and angered – knew that I must write the story of the Palestinian tragedy in a form that would be popularly read, and conceived the idea of the novel, *The Road to Beersheba*, published in 1963. At the end of 1962 I was back in Jericho with Musa Alami collecting material for this book, designed as an 'answer' to the Zionist novel, *Exodus*, mine to be the story of the *other* exodus – the enforced exodus of a million Palestinians, an entire nation, for the establishment of 'Israel', at the heart of the Arab homeland, against the impassioned expressed wishes of the *indigenous* people, the Palestinians. The novel was translated into Arabic, run as a serial in a Jordanian newspaper, and given as a serial over the Voice of the Arabs radio. How it was proposed by the Jordanians and the Egyptians to make it into a film I have told in *Stories from my Life*. I called the chapter *Making a Film with the Arabs*. The film, in fact, was never made, but it was an interesting and exciting experience whilst it lasted – not making a film with the Arabs.

As a result of meeting with a remarkably brilliant young Palestinian in the huge Ein-es-Sultan refugee camp outside Jericho I conceived the idea of writing a second Palestinian novel, this one to speak for the resistance – then illegal, except through Syria – as *The Road to Beersheba* had spoken for the refugees, and I wrote *The Night and its Homing*, published in 1966. This, also, was translated into Arabic, the work being carried out whilst I was in Damascus, on my last visit to the Middle East, in November 1966.

In 1963, 1964 and 1965, I was in and out of Amman and Cairo continuously. In 1964 I published a book about Egypt, which I called *Aspects of Egypt*, and which included an account of my interview with President Nasser at his house outside Cairo. The following year I published a book about Jordan, which I called *The Lovely Land*. I wrote nothing as a result of my visit to Syria in 1966, except for the account of a curious incident beside the Barada river, of which I wrote in *Stories from my Life*. I had a strenuous ten days in Syria on that second official visit, meeting the Head of State, the Prime Minister, government officials, visiting schools, co-operatives, villages, speaking at the university, being interviewed, meeting members of women's organizations, going north to Aleppo and Lattakia; it was exhausting, but it was all very interesting; they had much to show me and much socialistic achievement to be proud of, yet though I kept a detailed journal I did not feel that I wanted to write about Ba'athist Syria; the regime was too doctrinaire for my political taste, and there were aspects of it which I did not like – the National Guard, and young village girls in uniform. Also, I was not alone in thinking at that time that the government was shaky. However, ten years later the regime is unchanged – though even had I known that it would be I could not have written the book they hoped for from me. In *A Lance for the Arabs*, in 1962, I had written all I felt I wanted to write about Syria, and I still felt this in 1966. Of Damascus I recorded in my journal that it was 'a very beautiful city, with its woods, the Ghouta (the word means garden) girdling it, and its tree-lined streets and handsome balconied houses. There are no hideous high blocks, no Americanization. The setting, surrounded by hills, and orchards of orange, lemon, peach trees, is beautiful, and there is the little Barada river, only part of which has been covered over (in 1962 there was the threat to cover it all in).' I wrote of Damascus at some length in *A Lance*, but in 1966 I was not being shown Syria historically or scenically, but politically.

Now, nearly ten years later, there are two Syrian memories

about which I want to write in this context of 'the time of my life'.

I was driven by the military to the frontier town of Kuneitra – the frontier, that is to say, with Israel. It is up in the hills, the Golan Heights, and always referred to as The Frontier. It is an hour and a half's drive from Damascus. At Kuneitra, at the Officers' Club, there was a coffee session with the Colonel, and then we continued on to a point in the hills above the Sea of Galilee, which is in Israel, and from which we looked across to the villages and kibbutzim of Occupied Palestine. The hill scenery here is extremely beautiful, and I had last seen the Sea of Galilee from the Jordan side, looking down on to the little spa town of Hama. Later we drove down to Hama, lush and green as an oasis, with scarlet-blossomed trees and banana trees, like Jericho, and like Jericho below sea-level. It was very warm down there, and smelt of the sulphur baths. Before this descent, however, we stood high in the hills and looked across the valley to a group of trees from which, it was explained to me, came 'the Israeli aggression'. Though no Israeli soldiers were to be seen, an officer assured me the hills were full of them, and pointed out some half-concealed dugouts. All the villagers in this area, I was told, were trained and armed.

We then drove to the cemetery in Kuneitra, in which the soldiers and civilians who have died in the Frontier skirmishing are buried. I had thought the Al-Asifa guerillas might be buried there, but was told, no, only Syrians. We stopped in front of a memorial to the Unknown Soldier, and here I was given a wreath bearing my name inscribed in Arabic on a purple sash and asked to lay it on the steps. This, with a little assistance – it was a large and heavy wreath – I did, and when it was laid we all stood to attention as the Last Post was sounded ... than which there can be no more poignantly melancholy sound in the world. It was profoundly moving, and we returned to our cars, as the last note died away, in a silence made up of sorrow and anger. No photographs were taken; so many photographs had been taken of all that I did, press photographs and television, but none were taken there. Here was only grief and bitterness and tribute. I was proud to have been given the privilege of laying the wreath, and could have wept; and innerly did.

That night I was taken in a Volkswagen to a bleak and bare apartment where I met some of the Al-Asifa people and had the Al-Fatah movement explained to me. It was all very secretive, with no names, and I have no idea where I was taken, but despite this they spoke freely of their aims and strategy, which at that time, before 1967 and the emergence of Al-Fatah into the open as the spear-head of the Resistance, was a measure of their trust, and as moving an experience as the laying of the wreath.

It seems strange, now, that I never wrote about all this until some ten years later – not even in *Stories from my Life.* It was, I can only suppose, because I had resolved not to write about Ba'athist Syria, though any mention in the press or on the radio of fighting on the Golan Heights immediately poignantly recalls the lament of the Last Post reverberating through the cemetery of Kuneitra.

The other Syrian memory of which I now want to write is of walking beside the Mediterranean at Lattakia, discussing *Hamlet* with the young Syrian journalist who was my escort and interpreter. The morning sunshine was warm and bright, the sea Midi blue, and there was a feeling of intense happiness such as comes only rarely and is inexplicable – out of all proportion to the importance of the event that inspires it. I should have liked to have spent all the morning just walking and talking with that pleasant and intelligent young man beside the blue sea, but it was only a brief interlude before the day's official programme, which began with a call on the Governor, to be followed by a visit to a National Guard secondary school for girls, and then I had to be shown the new port. But how blessed that short interval of relaxation, how strangely happy . . . beyond all reason. I was never in Syria again, or anywhere in the Middle East.

In 1965 I was in Cairo in February, and again in March for the great Palestine Conference at the university, and I went on with the other delegates to Jerusalem. I was back there in April for a Palestinian friend's wedding – of which I wrote in *The Lovely Land*, in a chapter entitled *A Jordanian Wedding*.

So much for the record of my Middle East journeyings of the first half of the sixties, and the books they produced; what I also want to record are the Arab friendships of those years, the deeply felt emotional involvement. On arrival at Amman airport I was always met by a Palestinian friend who whisked me away in his car to his house, where his wife and daughters would have prepared a sumptuous meal of innumerable dishes, as is the Arab fashion. With this friend and members of his family I would drive up to Jerusalem on a Friday, the Muslim sabbath, to visit his mother who lived just outside. There we would have an enormous lunch of many dishes, and sometimes I would sit with the women picking over the rice before cooking, taking out the unripe grains. This family were refugees from Lydda in the summer of 1948, when the Palestinians were expelled from there – and from neighbouring villages – and turned out into the burning desert to trek to Ramallah in Jordan; they were not allowed by the military to use the roads, and as Sir John Bagot Glubb (Glubb Pasha) wrote in his fine book, *A Soldier with the Arabs*,* 'We shall never know how many children died.' It was of this terrible journey that I wrote in *A Road to Beersheba* – and did not tell all that was told to me by this family and others who had been on that trek for fear of seeming to exaggerate . . . of which I was anyhow accused. Members of this family, including the old mother, became refugees for the second time in June 1967.

But those were the good days, going up to Jerusalem, to Arab Jerusalem, on Fridays, from Amman, and driving up to it sometimes in the hot evenings from Jericho, with a member of that same Alami family. I loved Jericho, over eight hundred feet below sea-level, 'at the bottom of the basin' of which the Judean hills formed the rim; Jericho with its date-palms and banana trees and bougainvillea flaming over ancient walls, Jericho with its great dominating hulk of the Mount of Temptation – tempting one to ascend it, which of course one did – pausing halfway at the mona-stery; Jericho with Elisha's spring, from which the women draw water as in Biblical times – but these graceful figures in their flowing dresses, balancing pitchers and petrol cans on

* 1957.

their heads, are, alas, from the huge refugee camp just outside the town, at the foot of the Mount of Temptation, the Ein-es-Sultan camp, where over 18 000 Palestinians live one-room-to-a-family, and have done since 1948, existing on U.N.W.R.A. subsistence-level rations and waiting to return to their homes and lands in Jaffa, Haifa, Nazareth, Lydda, Beersheba, and many other towns and villages in what since 1948 has been 'Israel'. Jericho of the brown desert hills, the desert stretching away to the flat, sultry Dead Sea; Jericho of the squalid little town with the shabby neon-lit cafés at which men wearing the traditional Arab robes and head-dress sit interminably smoking their water-cooled pipes and drinking thick sweet Turkish coffee, and listening to the plaintive voice of Um Kalthun, Star of the East, the Egyptian singer – who died this year, 1975 – over the radio. They could never have enough of her and her sweet melancholy of love and longing. Well, that was Jericho, with the almost unendurable daytime heat, down there at the bottom of the basin, and the hot, airless nights . . . when it was so wonderful to drive up into the relative cool of Jerusalem.

I am glad to have known East Jerusalem whilst it was Arab. There was the dividing wall, to be sure, and the desolation of No Man's Land between it and Israeli West Jerusalem; it was a tragically divided city, and with bitterness my Palestinian friends and I would look across to the ugly modern building 'over there' in what we always referred to as Occupied Territory. But in Arab Jerusalem there was the wonderful Dome of the Rock, the Old City, the ancient Damascus Gate set in the massive city walls, the narrow, winding Via Dolorosa, the Church of the Holy Sepulchre, and just outside the city, as you climbed up from Jericho, the Mount of Olives, with the Garden of Gethsemane, its church, and the old gnarled olive trees, and the view along the Kedran Valley to the pale distant glimmer of the Dead Sea, and the shadowy-misty Mountains of Moab. Below the Ecce Homo convent, under an archway on the Via Dolorosa, there is the Roman pavement of what was Pilate's headquarters – stones on which Jesus himself stood at his trial.

I wrote of it all in *The Lovely Land,* and it is all still there, but since 1967 Israeli modernization has encroached upon it all, with modern blocks on Mount Scopus; it is no longer a divided city; it is unified – but Occupied. Like lush, exotic Jericho. Like Bethlehem. Like all of what was once the ancient land of Palestine, for two thousand years a continuously inhabited Arab country. *Le plus ça change* does not apply here; for the more it changes the more it becomes modernized, Westernized, vulgarized, and, as Jerusalem the Golden, lost.

Baghdad I liked and was excited by, and Cairo I came to know intimately and to love. At the airport I would always be met by an Egyptian friend – the lawyer of whom I wrote in *Making a Film with the Arabs* – and the first night of my return we would invariably celebrate by dining at one of the house-boat restaurants on the Nile. Very fine it was, too, to take tea, or drinks, on the terrace of the old Semiramis Hotel beside the Nile, watching the tremendous sunset over the massed palm trees at the other side, in the residential area of Zamalik. I have walked all over Cairo, in all directions, and by doing so really came to know the city, in all its aspects. In the evenings I would sit with my Egyptian friend in the Night and Day café of the Semiramis, much frequented by Cairo journalists, or on the roof at Shepherd's Hotel, after which we would have a meal somewhere – 'dine' was often too grand a word. Sometimes we would eat at one of the pigeon restaurants along the Nile – so-called because only pigeon was served there. The grilled pigeon, with a bottle of Egyptian wine – from the vineyards around Alexandria – was always good, and it would be pleasant beside the Nile, in the cool of evening, particularly when it was in flood and brimming, but the occasions would be spoiled by the hordes of starving cats prowling around the tables, waiting for scraps to be flung to them.

The Nile is ever present in Cairo – to be strolled along in the blessed cool of evening, to be dined on, occasionally, in a house-boat restaurant, to view a sunset from, or enjoyed in the freshness of early morning from a hotel balcony, with an exciting view across the desert to the Pyramids in the near distance, dim with the already rising heat-haze. I love Cairo, as I loved Jericho, and as I loved Arab Jerusalem.

I did not love Amman, a straggling and dusty and characterless city built on dusty desert hills, but I had good and dear Palestinian friends there, and it was always exhilarating to go with them down to the heat of Jericho or up to the cool of Jerusalem. From Amman, too, I was three times taken to the incredible rock-hewn city of Petra, 400 B.C. and Nabatean, and which T. E. Lawrence, visiting it in 1914, declared was the 'most wonderful place in the world'. But he also declared that the narrow gorge, the Siq, which is the entrance to it, was 'only just wide enough for a camel at a time', when in fact it is wide enough for a big Chevrolet truck or a broad American car, in both of which I have been through it. Cars are not allowed into the Siq, but when I was taken through by truck and by car I was an official guest and had no choice. The usual approach is by foot or on horseback; tourists love to go through on horseback, led by eager Arab boys, but it is in fact perfectly easy to walk through, though rough-going, calling for strong shoes or boots. I wrote of Petra at some length in *The Lovely Land*, so will add no more here except to say that these visits to this astonishing place were high spots in the time of my life, bracketed, perhaps, with the visit to the wonderful desert ruins of Palmyra in Syria. Blessed are mine eyes. . . .

But this I felt so many times – almost all the time – in Jordan, which is, mostly truly, the 'lovely land'. Memory fifteen years later, endorses – with intense nostalgia – all that I wrote in 1962:* 'This land called Jordan is of a quite incredible beauty, particularly west of the river, the part which was once Palestine. It is scenery done on a broad screen, the arc of the sky very wide, the horizons infinitely far, a landscape of immense panoramas continually viewed from above as the road snakes round high hills. The valleys are very deep, the hills very high, and the plains flow away in all directions, like vast seas, to the very edge of the world, it seems. To drive from Amman, on the east bank of the river, to Jericho, on the west bank, is to drive down through

* In *A Lance for the Arabs*.

the mountains and the Jordan Valley, through wildly beautiful country, with orange and lemon groves and cultivated
land that once was desert. Much of it is still semi-desert, with
outcrops of red rock and great boulders, and bare hillsides
covered with scrub and clumps of wild tulip, and everywheıe
among the stones the scarlet and mauve of wild anemones,
and the delicate pink of cyclamen. There has been a good
deal of afforestation, providing dark patches on the grey-
green landscape flowing away to ranges of blue hills and the
immensely far horizon.'

It was always an intense happiness to drive through the
Jordan Valley, just as it was an unfailing uplift of the heart
to drive up to Jerusalem, the 'city set on an hill', with the
sudden sight of the spires and towers crowning the sweep of
the hill, high and distant and somehow unexpected. There
was always that catch of the breath, the heart and mind
exulting, 'Ah! Jerusalem!' The Jerusalem skyline, the great
range of the Judean hills, near at last, and the other way the
Mountains of Moab folding into each other in the blue
distance. Quoth the raven, Nevermore! But it was something
to have seen, not once, but many times; to have experienced.
For it was more than merely a beholding with the outward
eye.

Just as, in Iraq, were the remaining bricks of Babylon,
with Nebuchadnezzar's inscriptions, 'Nebuchadnezzar, King
of Babylon, son of Nabopolassar, King of Babylon am I'.
The ruins of Babylon, and Nineveh, buried under the sand,
unexcavated, so that you walk over temples and palaces and
city walls, all that worldly pomp and splendour, against
which the Biblical Nahum raged, now nothing but a few
grass-grown mounds; and Ur-of-the-Chaldees, with its
astonishing staged tower, the *ziggurat*, fifty feet high, and
older than Babylon's Tower of Babel, of which nothing now
remains. It is something to have walked amongst the ruins
of Babylon, and over the mounds of buried Nineveh, and
to have climbed the terraces of the *ziggurat* of Ur-of-the-
Chaldees.

Indeed, it is very much, and Iraq alone would have
constituted 'the time of my life' in 1962, but then, and in the
following Middle East years, there was much else, not least

the Nubian adventure, which was a nightmare of heat, flies, dehydration, dysentery, and, because there were no wells in some of the villages, drinking water straight from the Nile. It was a horror, but it was intense living. It was experience with a capital E.* It was all part of a time when I was living intensely every moment of my waking hours, was never lonely – as on so many of my travels – and had the satis-faction of knowing it was all material for books which I hoped and believed would serve the cause I had so deeply at heart.

To enjoy what one is doing and believe it to be useful, that surely is an experience which adds up to the time of anyone's life.

---

* I wrote about it in *Aspects of Egypt*, 1964, and in a novel with a Cairo and Nubian background, *The Burning Bush*, 1965.

15

Re-reading Conrad and others

George Gissing read enormously, and in his quasi-auto-biographical *The Private Papers of Henry Ryecroft* he makes the retired writer, 'Henry Ryecroft', happily relieved of the burden of writing, exult in the thought that now he 'can sit reading, quietly reading, all day long', and when he is not walking in the Devon countryside or writing his reflective 'papers', a kind of journal, this is what he does. I do not, myself, sit reading all day long, since there are the domestic chores, shopping, gardening, correspondence, to attend to – not to mention a book to write; nor do I walk in the countryside, except to show the occasional visitor the local scene. But I do read a good deal – mostly in bed late at night, which has been my habit for many years. And since I came to Devon I re-read *Henry Ryecroft*, which excited me in my youth and speaks very much to my condition in old age, along with Gissing's *Letters to Members of his Family*, which I had not previously read. In his preface to *Henry Ryecroft* Gissing describes Henry Ryecroft's 'cottage near Exeter', with its 'fine view across the valley of the Exe to Haldon', which is surely a description of his own house in Exeter, 'a plain little house amid its half-wild garden'.

Gissing I re-read because I was writing about writers in Devon, but Conrad I re-read all the time, and have done for years; whenever I had nothing else to read I always fell back on Conrad, and I still do, and since I came to Devon had the immense good fortune to discover seven of his stories which I had not previously read, six of them collected into a volume under the title, *A Set of Six*, first published in 1920 and re-issued in Dent's Collected Edition in 1954, and last reprinted in 1961. The seventh story is the famous *Amy Foster*, published in *Typhoon and Other Stories* in 1903, which volume was reprinted many times, and twice in 1973, by Penguin, when it was done in one volume with *The Nigger of the Narcissus*. I missed it because I read *Typhoon* – years ago – in *Tales of Unrest*, which did not include it. I heard – or read – a reference to it in connexion with radio, was astonished I had missed it, and tracked it down.

It is a tragic and terrible story, very upsetting, and as Jocelyn Baines wrote in his definitive critical biography of Conrad,* is important in that it 'vividly and simply illustrates one of the main themes of Conrad's work, the essential isolation and loneliness of the individual'. It is the story of a young Carpathian mountain peasant who set out to emigrate to America, enticed by an unscrupulous American employment agency, and who is shipwrecked off the English coast. He reaches the shore and takes refuge in a barn, after being rejected by the local people on whose doors he has knocked because he is utterly foreign to them and they take him for a madman. The only person who was not afraid of him, and who showed him compassion, was Amy Foster, the farmer's dull-witted servant, who brought him bread, had her hand kissed by him in gratitude, and who had, as Conrad says, 'enough imagination to fall in love'. She eventually marries him and they have a child – a son, to whom Yanko, the father, aspires to teach his own language, religion, songs. Amy resents this and they become alienated. All that had originally attracted her to him, his strangeness, comes to repel her, and when he falls ill – of what would seem to be pneumonia – and cries out deliriously in his own language, begging for water, she is overcome with terror, snatches up the child and rushes out into the night, fleeing the three-miles-and-a-half to her parents' cottage. The country doctor who narrates the story – in many of Conrad's stories there is a narrator – found Yanko next morning lying face down in a puddle outside the wicker gate of the cottage he had shared with Amy. He had rushed out after her and collapsed. The doctor carries him into the house and calls out for Amy.

* *Joseph Conrad, a Critical Biography*, 1959.

Yanko opens his eyes and says, distinctly, 'Gone!' adding, 'I had only asked for water – only a little water . . . ' He dies, and the doctor certifies heart-failure as the immediate cause of his death, but he died, the doctor suggests, more of a broken heart, perishing, as Conrad writes, 'in the supreme disaster of loneliness and despair'. As Osborn Andreas says in his book, *Joseph Conrad, a study in nonconformity*,* Yanko was 'a casualty to the provincialism characteristic of much group-life, to the prejudice of the homogeneous group against the outsider, and to that tendency of group members to close ranks upon the approach of an immigrant. Group exclusiveness in the abstract is clearly the villain of the story.'

Amy Foster is not only a powerful, moving human drama, but is of interest in that it has a degree of the autobiographical since Conrad himself came to England as an immigrant not knowing a word of the language, and the loneliness Yanko felt, lying in his emigrant bunk in the ship to England, Conrad himself must have felt. He makes the narrator of the story observe that 'it is indeed hard upon a man to find himself a lost stranger, helpless, incomprehensible, and of a mysterious origin, in some obscure corner of the earth'. Baines mentions that Bertrand Russell, who knew Conrad, cited this story in his book *Portraits from Memory and other Essays*,† 'as a key to Conrad's character'.

I wrote at some length about Conrad's inner loneliness in my book, *Loneliness, a Study of the Human Condition*,‡ and do not wish to be repetitive, but reading *Amy Foster* here in my Devon retirement, and profoundly moved by it, brought back to me what I wrote in that book, almost ten years ago, of Conrad as what Herman Melville called an *isolato*, one of those who inhabit a separate continent of their own, as Melville himself did – 'Call me Ishmael', says the narrator in the opening words of *Moby Dick* – remote from the common continent. Dr Adam Gillon, himself like Conrad, Polish-born, entitled his biography of Conrad, *The Eternal Solitary*,§ and says of him that 'since his experience as sailor and writer only enhanced the condition of loneliness, to which Conrad was disposed by his background and tempera-

* 1959.   † 1956.   ‡ 1966.   § 1960, New York.

ment, it is small wonder that his work shows a veritable procession of *isolatos*'. The *isolato* theme begins in his first novel, *Almayer's Folly*, published in 1895, in which Almayer is lonely and isolated because he marries a 'native', and is thus despised by the whites, and rejected by the natives because he is white.

But guilt is also a Conrad theme – guilt for something real or imagined – stemming from Conrad's own suppressed sense of guilt from running away from Poland, to go to sea, at a time when it was an intensely unpatriotic thing to do, but he was unwilling either to live under the Russian conquerors or to take part in futile resistance. As Andreas says, 'He chose instead to shake the dust of Poland from his feet, to break all ties with the people among whom he had been born and raised, and to take up the life of a sailor on all the oceans of the earth.' But the subconscious sense of guilt remained, and when he became a writer, in the English tongue he had so brilliantly acquired, the guilt emerged in story after story – the guilt and the ethical conflict; the guilt theme and the outcast theme.

Lord Jim, published in 1915, has the guilt theme plus expiation. This was my first Conrad novel; I bought it in 1916, when I was sixteen and working as a junior typist in an advertising agency, and I still have the battered old copy, published by William Blackwood, badly foxed and with its spine peeling, and for some reason, a twopenny tram ticket inside it as bookmark. What led me to Conrad I cannot now remember; perhaps I merely picked it up on a bookstall and thought it looked interesting – I liked tales of the sea because of my father's Jack London and W. W. Jacobs collection in the sevenpenny Nelson classics. But the novel enthralled me – as it did re-reading it fifty and sixty years later. It is the most symbolic of all Conrad's novels, for Jim's jump from his sinking ship into a boat is a clear symbol of Conrad's desertion of the sinking ship that was Poland. Yet Jim, no more than Conrad, was guilty only in his own mind – though the tribunal of inquiry to which Jim submitted himself censured him for conduct unbecoming to a ship's officer, and Conrad never overcame his guilt-complex – as his work witnesses. The narrator of the story is Marlow, a sea-captain, and a solitary, and Conrad's *altⱼr ego*. He first appears in *Youth*, a *Blackwood's Magazine* story of 1902, and is also the narrator of the dark and terrible and wonderful *Heart of Darkness* which followed, Conrad's favourite work, and surely one of the finest stories in the English language. I have read it several times, and within recent years.

But *Victory*, which I regard as Conrad's greatest novel, and which I first read in my Connemara cottage in the 'fifties, I have never re-read – the first experience was so shattering (like the first reading of Corvo's *The Desire and Pursuit of the Whole*) that I have never dared to. I was horrified to learn, a few years ago, that it had been made into an opera. There comes into this novel, as into *Amy Foster*, the tragic inability of two people, a man and a woman, living closely, intimately, devotedly, in mutual tenderness, really to come close to each other. The man, Heyst, does sincerely love the woman, but he cannot go out to her, and she cannot reach him because of his withdrawnness. Finally, in a situation of high drama and tragedy, she saves his life at the cost of her own and dies in exultant happiness, but for Heyst there is no solution but to follow her into death. He sets fire to the bungalow, making of it a funeral pyre for himself. The narrator of the story comments, 'I suppose he couldn't stand his thoughts before her dead body – and fire purifies everything.'

The *Set of Six* stories which I read recently for the first time, though I counted them a find, since they were new to me, are relatively unimportant, and from his Author's Note to them it would seem that Conrad himself did not rank them very highly. They were, he wrote, in 1920, the 'result of some three or four years' occasional work', and none of them connected directly with personal experiences, though 'the facts are inherently true' and 'they have actually happened'. *The Brute*, which he calls An Indignant Tale, is the only sea story in the collection; the 'brute' is a ship which nobody loved and which men preferred not to sail in; a ship that was 'mad', so that 'under no circumstances could you be sure she would do what any other sensible ship would do for you' . . . and she came to a sticky end. Jessie Conrad, in her biography of her husband, *Joseph Conrad as I Knew Him,**

* 1926.

says that Conrad told his publisher (in a letter to Sir Algernon Methuen, 26 January 1908) that the six stories 'are not studies – they touch no problem. They are just stories in which I've tried my best to be *simply entertaining*.' Ethical considerations come into them, nevertheless, but they are not, for me, stories to be re-read.

Nostronomo, published in 1904, and which Osborn Andreas considers 'the greatest creation of his career', 'the apex of his lifework, the very pinnacle of Conrad's achievement', I have so far failed to be able to read. Jocelyn Baines wrote that it was Conrad's most ambitious feat of imagination and worthy of comparison with 'the most ambitious of all great novels, *War and Peace*.' Baines has criticism of it – weakness of characterization, melodrama in the last two chapters 'inappropriately magazinish language,' but regarded it as 'perhaps Conrad's greatest sustained achievement'. He says of it that it is 'an intensely pessimistic book; it is perhaps the most impressive monument to futility ever created', and that in it Conrad 'portrayed the world as he saw it, not as he hoped it might become'. Conrad himself regarded the book as 'more of a Novel, pure and simple', than anything he had done since *Almayer's Folly*, and 'very genuine Conrad'. For me, attempting to get interested in it, this is precisely what it is not, for it is a political novel about a fictitious state created by revolution, to which the central character comes to mine silver. I could not get interested in it because the characters did not come alive for me and I found it hardgoing. Perhaps when I am tired of re-reading the familiar Conrad I will try again. *Nostronomo* is a long novel, and in general I do not like long novels. Though I did read *War and Peace* – skipping the war chapters.

Re-reading Conrad with the piece for this book in mind led me to look again at another old favourite, H. M. Tomlinson, whose novel *Gallions Reach*, published in 1927, made a profound impression on me when it was first published. Tomlinson met Conrad and had a tremendous admiration for his work. In his volume of travel memories, 'of ships, coasts, and chance companions', *Gifts of Fortune*,* he wrote

* 1926.

of receiving the news of Conrad's death at Chesil Bank, that
long beach which joins the Portland pensinsula to the main-
land, when he was living in a house on the moorland above
the Bank. Until then the Bank had for him 'no message'. It
was just 'a white-washed wall topped by a tamarisk hedge',
and below the wall 'a deserted ridge and beach of shingle,
tawny and glowing, and a wide sea without a ship'. It was all,
he wrote, as far from his own interests 'as a West Indian cay'.
Then, on 3 August 1924, a distant figure appeared on the
shingle, something so unusual that he watched it from two
miles away. The figure moved with briskness and determination and appeared to be unconcerned with anything on the
strand. It came straight to him as though it knew he was there
It proved to be a smiling and rosy-cheeked telegraph boy
from the post office three miles distant. The boy handed him
a telegram and Tomlinson opened it wondering 'who was in
such a hurry to announce some good fortune'. The message
was cryptic: *Conrad is dead*. Tomlinson tells us that he could
only stare at the messenger feeling that there must be more
to come. The boy asked, 'Anything to go back?' and
Tomlinson replied, 'No, nothing to go back.' But when the
first shock had worn off realized that, yes, there was something to go back – gratitude for Conrad's life and work;
there was that to go back.

Tomlinson found Conrad unknowable, even through his
work. 'There was something in him not to be clearly dis-
cerned. It was sought in his books with curiosity, but it did
not appear to be there. The man was only partly seen, as
through a veil. . . . Occasionally he would vouchsafe a
closer glimpse of himself, something to make us alert, but at
once fade into his own place.'

The first book of Conrad's which Tomlinson read was
The Nigger of the Narcissus, which Conrad called A Tale of the
Forecastle, and with his own firsthand knowledge of clipper
ships recognized it – as he says in his Chesil Bank essay – as
the real thing, such as he had never expected to see. From
this novel it was plain to him that the writer – whom he had
been told was a Pole – 'had added to the body of English
literature'. He added that as for *Youth* – which followed
Lord Jim, in 1902, and is one of Conrad's Shorter Tales – 'it

is, without doubt, one of the finest short narratives in the language, and there will never be again such a yarn of such a voyage in such a ship'.

Tomlinson wrote that in 1926, when he had yet to write *Gallions Reach*, and I do not know whether it has ever been suggested that this is 'pure Conrad', but in my opinion it is – not in any plagiaristic sense, no, certainly not, but in spirit; in essence.

Has it significance that the hero of *Gallions Reach* is called Jim? An unconscious reflection of *Lord Jim*? Perhaps. Jim Colet of Tomlinson's novel worked for an unpleasant importer called Perriam, whose office was in the City of London, in the area between Fenchurch Street and Leadenhall Street. Perriam had been master and part-owner of an opium clipper – an opium smuggler. In the City he imported mace, tumeric, cinnamon, and so forth, which 'were but names and markets to Colet. . . . So were the names of the ships which brought over the stuff, names of eastern cities and countries. . . . There was not a whisper of the voyages of the ships, except a rare call from the river when he was working late, the city was quiet, and the wind was south-west and wet.' Colet saw Perriam as 'an artful old hog' and a 'predatory monster'. He felt there must be another sort of life beyond that of the Perriams of the world 'if a fellow were only bold enough to smash the cage which had got him', coupled with the reflection that his cage might be smashed for him anyway. 'Perriam wouldn't think twice about it, if he were in the mood.' As it turns out he smashes the cage himself, one evening, after hours, at the office, when Perriam abuses him for not settling a dispute with his warehousemen; Perriam wants them all sacked; Colet refuses to be involved – they were good men and it was a matter for the union. Perriam rants and raves and accuses Colet of being a fraud, cheating the people who pay him. He raises an arm 'in trenchant reprobation'. Colet suddenly feels an upsurge of abhorrence that turns him black. 'He saw Perriam's near mask as the front of all arrogant swinishness. He struck it.' Perriam falls to the floor, and to his astonishment Colet realizes that he doesn't rise from it because he is dead. He is dismayed and bewildered. 'Had he really hit his chief? He did not remember doing it. The violent old fool just dropped.' He thinks of going to the police, but he does not go. Instead he spends the night in a hotel in the City and in the morning, in the coffee room, falls in with the master of the *Altair*, about to sail for the China Sea. Colet sails in this ship inadvertently, as a result of doing the captain a small service by taking a statuette of the goddess Kuan-yin – for whom he has himself a veneration – to the ship. The launch leaves without him. He has a chance later of going ashore, but does not take it. He does not know the destination of the ship. 'It was incidental. They were outward bound. Enough for one day; and one day at a time.' The ship is wrecked; there is a spell in an open boat, rescue by a liner, arrival in Rangoon. In the liner he meets a passenger called Norrie who is off to a Malayan jungle expedition and who persuades Colet to accompany him. He is a prospector, strictly non-metaphysical, not in the least Colet's kind of person, but Colet is a destitute seaman about to be landed in Rangoon, and he accepts the proposition. From Rangoon he and Norrie travel by coaster to Penang and Colet begins 'to hear from himself again'. Rangoon, with its 'slow flux of multitudinous people' had been 'just like the tide home-coming over London Bridge for the trains, moving to a compulsion which was as dark as its nature as a starless patch in the clear sky of night'. The two men make a long jungle journey together and Norrie discovers tin – his Holy Grail. There is another jungle journey, with an old and distinguished ethnologist, and final return to Penang – and here he meets Sinclair, chief officer of the *Altair*, sailing back to London the next day to Gallions Reach. Colet asks Sinclair to take him back with him. Sinclair, who knows about the killing of Perriam whom he, also, had detested, says that Colet can't mean it. But Colet insists that he has a ghost to lay – the ghost of Perriam. Sinclair says he would see his ghost in hell first. Colet replies that it's not really Perriam's ghost he has to lay but his own, adding that 'there's no fun for us unless we obey the order we know'. He sails back to Gallions Reach with Sinclair in order to give himself up.

This is the pure Conrad theme of guilt and expiation –

with shipwreck and Malaya thrown in for full measure. Jim Colet was no more criminal than Lord Jim, since he did not intend to kill Perriam, but as with Lord Jim there is the over-riding sense of guilt and the need for absolution by paying, ultimately, the penalty. *Gallions Reach* is an extremely complex book, full of metaphysical speculations, but I found it as fascinating and as powerful re-reading it in 1975 as when I first read it in 1927.

My admiration for Cunninghame Graham, Tschiffely's 'Don Roberto', began long before I had read anything he had written; his was one of the great names of my socialist upbringing, along with John Burns and Keir Hardie – with both of whom he was associated in their early days. That he was an aristocrat made his socialism all the more admirable. I read Tschiffely's biography, *Don Roberto*, published in 1937, a year after Cunninghame Graham's death, and my youthful interest in his very remarkable personality was revived, but except for his preface to Conrad's posthumously published *Tales of Hearsay, and Last Essays*, and his own little book of tales and essays, *Faith*, which I read in the re-issued edition in 1929, I do not think I ever read anything of his. I am inclined to agree with Jocelyn Baines that he was 'never primarily a writer, let alone an artist', and that his work is in the borderland between fiction and non-fiction – certainly that contained in *Faith* is; it is a collection of pieces rather than anything specifically tale or essay.

In his time he was revolutionary, which makes his friendship with Conrad, who was almost rabidly anti-revolutionary, all the more curious. Conrad regarded Cunninghame Graham as 'a hopeless idealist', but he was intensely grateful for his appreciation of his work and deeply valued it, and Cunninghame Graham for his part was enthusiastically appreciative of the implicitly anti-imperialist attitude expressed in Conrad's story, *An Outpost of Progress*, about which he wrote to him, and which was the beginning of their lifelong friendship. Conrad dedicated the long short story, *Typhoon*, to Cunninghame Graham. He told his publisher, Blackwood, that he did so not to the aristocrat or the socialist – 'he is both, you know' – but to one of the few men he really *knew*, 'in the full sense of the word, and knowing cannot but appreciate and respect', even though, he added, he did not share his political convictions or even all his ideas of art. They had, nevertheless, 'enough ideas in common to base a strong friendship upon'.

The story of which Cunninghame Graham thought so highly is not, to my mind, vintage Conrad. It is a squalid story of two white men whose 'outpost of progress' is a trading station in the Congo – Conrad called it 'the lightest part of the loot' he carried off from the Congo. Jocelyn Baines says of it that 'although it may not have the scope or power of *Heart of Darkness* (Conrad's only other story with the Congo as a setting) and again shows the influence of Maupassant it has a well-handled and original subject: the rapid disintegration of two white traders, average products of the machine of civilisation, when confronted with the corroding power of solitude and the unusual'. The two men get on each other's nerves, quarrel over a trivial matter, and as a result one shoots the other and then hangs himself. Conrad was pleased with the story and sent it to Edward Garnett declaring that it should be the first of a volume dedicated to him. It duly appeared in *Tales of Unrest*, published in 1898, but it was the third story in the volume and was not dedicated to Garnett – or anyone else – though the novel, *The Nigger of the Narcissus*, which Conrad was working on at the same time, and which was published the same year, was. In his author's note to *An Outpost of Progress* Conrad declared that the 'main portion' of the loot he carried off from the Congo was 'of course *The Heart of Darkness*'. Of *An Outpost* he said that it was 'true enough in essentials', adding that 'the sustained invention of a really telling lie demands a talent which I do not possess'. Which means that all of Conrad's stories are based on facts with which he was acquainted, or on personal experience.

Cunninghame Graham, in his preface to *Tales of Hearsay*, wrote that Conrad's first novel, *Almayer's Folly*, revealed him as a 'born story-teller'. He found no evidence of immaturity in the book – 'Conrad seems to have sprung, just as Minerva sprang, straight from Jove's brow, full armed and full equipped. His English is as perfect, perhaps more perfect, than in his latest work.' Cunninghame Graham maintained that 'as the years roll on a language that we have acquired in youth, when all our faculties are keen, and with the first impact that a strange tongue makes on the brain, gradually fades, and the speech that we learned at our mother's knee subconsciously reasserts itself.' He considered that *The Warrior's Soul*, the first story in *Tales of Unrest*, written in 1917, shows Conrad's genius as 'ever maturing, never looking back, as fresh and powerful as when, many years ago, he wrote those masterpieces, *The Heart of Darkness, Youth*, and *The Mirror of the Sea*'. He declared that few stories in the language were as dramatic as *The Warrior's Soul*, and that in it Conrad seemed to have put forth all his powers as a short-story writer. It was, he wrote, 'a sort of swan song, for though he added to his laurels with his last book, *The Rover*, as regards the short story, when he had written the last pages of *The Warrior's Soul* he laid the lyre aside for good.'

The Rover was not, in fact, Conrad's last book, nor even his last novel, for at the time of his death he had written some eighty thousand words of a novel, *Suspense*, which he described as a Napoleonic novel, and which, incomplete, was published in 1925, following serialization in the *Saturday Review of Literature*.

The Warrior's Soul, written in 1916, is a story of the retreat from Moscow; it is a powerfully written story, and as in so much of Conrad's work the question of ethics enters in. It is the story of a young Russian soldier, Tomassov, who had been attached to the embassy in Paris, where he fell in love with a woman of some social distinction. At her salon he eventually meets a French officer, De Castel, who warns him of the impending war, which, if it had overtaken him, would have meant his internment for the duration. Forewarned he has the opportunity to get out before it happens. He is overwhelmed with gratitude to De Castel and tells him that if he ever has the opportunity to repay him 'you may command my life'. Tomassov is grateful not only to have escaped internment in France but to get back to Russia to fight in the defence of his country against the French invasion, but his attitude to Frenchmen in general had been profoundly affected by De Castel's gesture. The old Russian

Top Widecombe-in-the-Moor: a fairly recent High Street commemoration of the famous ballad of Widecombe Fair

Above Chagford, old market town on the edge of Dartmoor: the old bakehouse in the High Street

Top Postbridge, Dartmoor: the 'clapper bridge' over the East Dart river, probably thirteenth century

Above Bellever, Dartmoor: the remains of a clapper bridge with the modern bridge behind

officer who is the narrator says, 'He was naturally indignant at the invasion of his country, but this indignation had no personal animosity in it. He grieved at the appalling amount of human suffering he saw all around him. Yes, he was full of compassion for all forms of mankind's misery in a manly way. Less fine natures than his did not understand this very well. In the regiment they had nicknamed him the Humane Tomassov.'

Tomassov took no offence at this, and the narrator observes that 'there is nothing incompatible between humanity and a warrior's soul'. It was important to make this point about Tomassov's sensitivity and humanity because eventually the French officer, De Castel, falls into Tomassov's hands as a prisoner-of-war, and, because through his suffering he has lost all faith and courage, begs Tomassov to shoot him and put an end to his mental and physical misery. For Tomassov it is an appalling request, apart from the fact that it is against the rules to shoot a prisoner-of-war, but when he hesitates De Castel is contemptuously angry and calls him a 'milksop', demanding hasn't he got the soul of a warrior? The anguish for Tomassov is not only that De Castel is in agony and screaming, '*Tuez moi! Tuez moi!*' but that he had promised the Frenchman that if ever he could do anything for him he would – that he had but to ask. Now he is faced with this terrible demand. After that final tormented jeer of 'milksop' he shoots – 'One warrior's soul paying its debt a hundredfold to another warrior's soul by releasing it from a fate worse than death – the loss of all faith and courage.' Tomassov pays for his act by standing accused of shooting a prisoner-of-war in cold blood. He is not dismissed from the service but after the war resigns from the army 'to bury himself in the depths of his province, where a vague story of some dark deed clung to him for years'.

That Cunninghame Graham should so greatly admire this story is understandable, for the essential greatness of Conrad's spirit is in it, rising above nationalisms. 'Even his hatred of the hereditary tyrants of his country is forgotten,' Cunninghame Graham writes. 'He sees them with their country laid waste and invaded by the Napoleonic hordes,

E

and as he understood by dire experience, what they were passing through gives them his sympathy. No light thing for a Pole to do . . .' He describes it as a most 'remarkable and dramatic story', and says of it that it was a hearsay tale, heard in Conrad's youth and written in his later years, 'when his thoughts turned again to old familiar things'.

Cunninghame Graham ended his preface to the *Tales of Hearsay* with a description of a fountain in Marrakesh, 'a gem of Moorish art', upon which was inscribed in Cufic characters the words, 'Drink and admire'. He commands that we should 'Read and admire; then return thanks to Allah who gives water to the thirsty and at long intervals sends us refreshment for the soul'.

Tomlinson cites this passage in his essay on the Chesil Bank with its account of his receiving by telegram the news of Conrad's death, and considering what there was to 'go back' in response to that telegram, and I like it so much that I make no apology for citing it myself. It contains the essence of what there is to go back in gratitude for Conrad's life and work.

Conrad suffered enormously in the production of his stories and novels, and the completion of a novel was usually accompanied by physical collapse. So that it is interesting to find Cunninghame Graham declaring in his preface to his own stories, 'Everything that a man writes brings sorrow to him of some kind or other. . . . Let nobody deceive himself . . . that books are spun out from the inner consciousness. . . . Such processes are well enough for silk worms, but men spin little silk from their own bowels, and still less from their brains. All that they write, even the sonnets, those of Shakespeare and of Keats, has cost them labour and much biting of pens. This is so, and artists of all kinds, whether in paint or letters, in marble, bronze, or in what medium they work, all know it thoroughly. . . . All that we write is but a bringing forth again of something we have seen or heard about. What makes it art is but the handling of it, and the imagination that is brought to bear upon the theme out of the writer's brain.'

Thus Cunninghame Graham wrote of his experiences and

observations in Spain, Morocco, Italy, Mexico, Paraguay, but mostly of Spain, his spiritual home – he was three-quarters Scottish and a quarter Spanish and declared that his outlook on life was and always had been Spanish. Jocelyn Baines comments, 'If his outlook really was Spanish it was that of a true *hidalgo* born out of his time. But perhaps he was more like an Elizabethan adventurer, such as Raleigh. . . .'

Like H. W. Nevinson he was in his time a militant radical, socialist, anti-imperialist, a champion of justice and freedom. He was also a great traveller and horseman. His life was spectacular, and with his striking handsomeness, and capacity for assuming a role, he was perhaps a flamboyant personality; certainly he was remarkable, and certainly he could write vividly of the scenes he knew and the people who inhabited those landscapes. As a writer he is the antithesis of Conrad and Tomlinson; there are no subtleties in his writing, no trace of any preoccupation with ethical or emotional conflicts; he is the complete extrovert. He wrote sketches rather than stories, and he calls his collection of pieces in *Faith* precisely that, written, he says, as clearly as his vision permitted.

There is no indication as to why the collection is called *Faith*; there is nothing of that title in the book, and nothing – that I can see – to link the pieces in a general theme that might be regarded as an expression of faith of some kind. Cunninghame Graham wrote in his preface, '. . . almost all of the stories, sketches, or what you choose to call them, in this book are sad. . . . In none of them is any moral drawn, or if it is, it is attempted to be drawn, it is set down as truthfully as possible . . . is it not better to write truthfully, when all is sad, than to write on sad things after the manner of your only jig-maker?' So the collection starts off with the sad story of *Sor Candida and the Bird*. Sister Candida is a nun in a convent in sun-scorched Avila. She rescues a bird dying of thirst and takes it into her cell and revives it, but instead of setting it free when it revives makes a little cage for it, and in this she keeps it for a year – 'not thinking for a moment that after giving life she thus would take away life's chiefest treasure – liberty!' It is against the rules for a nun to have a pet of any kind, distracting her from her allegiance to her spiritual husband, Christ, but the prioress condones it, as does the visiting provincial later. So the imprisoned bird grows fat and sings, and the nuns, enraptured, declare that to hear him sing was next to listening to the celestial choirs. A year passes and 'once again the short, but fierce Castilian summer heated the rocks of Avila'. It is the feast of the saint, and from dawn till evening the nuns are busy running up and down, decorating the church with flowers and attending services. In all this busyness the bird is neglected and dies of thirst. Filled with an anguish of remorse, mingled with contrition, Sister Candida declares that the death of her beloved 'little one' is a punishment that has perhaps come upon her 'as a warning that we nuns should not attach ourselves to anyone but Christ'.

It is the most moving piece in the book, and the only one with any real pretensions to being a story, in the sense that it has a beginning, a middle and an end. There is a sketch of an Arab funeral, and of Christmas week in the London of the period, with its smell of horse-dung and 'motor-omnibuses' disporting themselves 'like great Behemoth or Leviathan, reducing their creators to an inferior place, as if they lived upon the sufferance of the great whirring beasts'. There is a purely descriptive piece about the Pampa of Patagonia, 'a green illimitable sea, in which the horse was ship; a desert without camels, but as terrible to wander in as is the Sahara. . . .'

There is a sketch of cattle grazing their way to the slaughter-house, their calves frisking beside them; and of a painter, 'Dutch Smith', painting the church at Haarlem year in and year out; there is a long piece about Andorra, and another long piece about a medieval statue of a shepherd in a church at Toledo – closer to being travel sketches than anything else. There is a half-story called *Mektoub* about a blind beggar in Tangier whom a German doctor operates on in an attempt to restore his sight; the operation fails and the doctor weeps with grief and disappointment, but the beggar is philosophic; *Mektoub* – it was written that his sight should not be restored, and that is all there is to it. He urges the doctor not to weep. 'It was not written,' he says, and returns to his seat outside the principal hotel.

It was interesting to re-read this collection of pieces, but they did not provide the satisfaction of re-reading Conrad – they were too essentially 'external', whereas Conrad's stories are essentially 'inner', concerned with the conflicts of human psychology. For me Cunninghame Graham is better rememberd as a remarkable personality, an adventurer in the Elizabethan tradition – indeed, Tschiffely calls him 'the last of the Elizabethans – a great horseman, and a stalwart defender of freedom and justice'. He himself declared, in a letter to a publisher who wanted him to review a Masefield poem, that he could not do it because he was not *au fond*, as he put it, 'a man of letters', having only, he wrote, 'a mild connection with literature'. That was in 1912, and he had begun writing in 1899, when he was forty-seven, and until 1906 had produced a book a year, five of which were collections of short stories, but two of which, *A Vanished Arcadia*, and *Hernando de Soto*, dealing with Spanish and South American history, involved a good deal of research. From a travel and adventure book about Morocco, *Mogreb-El-Acksa*, published in 1899, G. B. Shaw admitted he got the local colour for his play, *Captain Brassbound's Conversion*. Wilfrid Scawen Blunt regarded this book as the equal of Doughty's *Arabia Deserta* 'as a true portrait of Arab ways, and far before anything that Burton did'. He added that it was a book he would read again. In 1904, after the publication of *Hernando de Soto*, Blunt wrote to Cunninghame Graham that he followed his literary fortunes 'with the greatest interest', seeing in him 'the only competititor to beat Kipling on his own ground'. Blunt was, of course, intensely opposed to British Imperialism. Tschiffely says of a sketch called *Niggers* that it was 'possibly the most indignant, satiric denunciation of English Imperialism that has ever been published', and Edward Garnett said of it that with its fellow-sketch, *Success*, it 'would confer immortality on him', if he had written nothing more. W. H. Hudson, a great friend of Cunninghame Graham's, declared him 'unique among English writers', adding that his 'singularity' was most evident when he wrote of people of other races, 'because of the union in you of two rare qualities – or the rare union of two qualities – intense individuality, and detachment, which enables you to identify even with those who are most unlike us'. Conrad sat up half the night reading *Hernando de Soto* and found it 'exquisitely excellent . . . the most amazingly natural thing I've ever read; it gives me a furious desire to learn Spanish and bury myself in the pages of the incomparable Garcilasso – if only to forget all about our modern Conquistadores'. In spite of all this high praise for Cunninghame Graham's writings from distinguished literary quarters, however, the British public, Tschiffely tells us, 'remained indifferent to them, and the sales of the books were very small'.

To a reader who wrote to him about his book, *José Antonio Páez*, criticizing the syntax and punctuation, though the book had had high praise from the literary reviews, Cunninghame Graham replied amiably that he was not 'a writer of repute', to which he added 'Praise Allah', adding that he did not live by writing – 'or I should have starved long ago' – and the punctuation was his own and if he altered it his writing 'would lose entirely'. He thought that some of the things his correspondent complained of were 'simply mistakes', and others he thought were Hispaniolisms – 'as I am practically bi-lingual'. He explained that 'to affront a journey' was an Hispaniolism, and he did not dislike it, using 'affront' in the sense of 'set face to'. He was entirely unoffended by the letter, and concluded it 'Yours with thanks'.

Like Conrad he was a great preface writer, and Conrad called him 'Prince of Preface-Writers', though personally I think the title goes to Conrad. 'Your Prefaces are so good!' Conrad wrote him, adding that 'It is quite an art by itself'. But Cunninghame Graham liked to insist that he was 'a mere dabbler' and an 'amateur', though he did enormous research for his historical studies. He prided himself that he never made an on-the-spot, written note – a habit he despised; he was nevertheless, says Tschiffely, scrupulously accurate, and observes that 'both in his travel books and histories his personality emanates to such an extent that they are neither travel nor history, but rather literature of a very exceptional type'.

His last book, *Mirages*, was published shortly before he died – in 1936, at the age of eighty-four, in Buenos Aires – and Tschiffely wrote the introduction for it. In this book he made it clear that in spite of defending primitive poor peoples he was not in the least romantic about the Noble Savage – 'I know quite well that he uses no poison gas or bombs, simply because he has not got them, and is constrained to do his level best with poison arrows, launched from blow-pipe or bow, and other poor devices hatched in his neolithic brain.' He observed, also, that 'Had it not been for the eruption of the Latins (2000 years ago) against all justice and in defiance of the League of Nations of those days, Britons, who were the Abyssinians of the first century, B.C., might have remained woad-painted, bathless, and in ignorance of Virgil, Horace, Ovid and Petronius Arbiter . . . content to rob upon the highway as there is no mention of a Stock Exchange in Caesar's "Commentaries". . . .'

On that last journey to Buenos Aires, when asked by reporters on his arrival what he was currently writing, he replied that he was just finishing a preface to Hudson's works and, when the reported to whom he said this asked what next, replied, 'Just the preface to my death.'

He dictated a letter to Tschiffely on 16 March 1936, four days before his death, telling him he had received a copy of *Mirages* and that he thought it made 'a very nice little book', and that the reproduction of his bust – by Epstein – on the cover was 'excellent'. He was ill with bronchitis and died on 20 March. It is interesting that *Mirages* is the story of an Englishman of good family, 'Charlie the Gaucho', who after an adventurous life in the South American pampas decided to return there, after some years in England, 'to die with his boots on'. Tschiffely says that the story about 'Charlie the Gaucho', whom he had known as a youth, made him decide to return to Buenos Aires to die on the old trails. He died, as he had lived, without benefit of clergy. He told the Argentinian doctor who attended him in his last days, 'Some people need religion like a wall to lean against, but I have never needed it.'

Sometime, I tell myself, I may unearth a copy of *Mirages* from a library and really discover Cunninghame Graham as a writer, but certainly I would agree with the old Scottish crofter who came down from the Highlands for the funeral, as Tschiffely tells us, and paid him the just tribute, 'Aye, he was a bonny fighter, an' a grand gentleman.'

Re-reading another staunch defender of freedom and justice, H. W. Nevinson, was easier because I had never 'lost touch' with him as I had with Cunninghame Graham, and he was an active part of my particular political scene in the 'thirties. He did not die until the end of 1941, in his eighties, in 'exile', as he half ironically called it, in the small Gloucestershire town of Chipping Camden, having been bombed out of his London home. He loved London, and though he appreciated the beauties of the country landscape, 'the hillside and the purple wood', London still was his 'earthly paradise' and 'home', and he longed for the noisy streets, the traffic, the human multitude, and vowed:

> '*I'll struggle back to London town again,*
> *Mix with the London crowd,*
> *Though shattered roofs pour down the rain*
> *And guns are loud.*'

He never did get back, and in his last, unfinished poem, which he entitled *Peace*, wrote of the rural scene and peace lying like a sun 'on the midland wold', and in his last essay, written only a month before he died, he was dreaming not of London but of the mountains he had known, from the Alps to the Himalayas, and of the English hills, Cross Fell and Helvellyn, and Langdale, 'lovliest of valleys.' He could still, in his old age, he wrote, lift up his eyes unto the hills, 'whence come my spiritual help and my finest joy'.*

In the 'thirties he was, to us of the Left, 'dear old Nevinson' who could always be relied on to champion a cause for justice and freedom for the oppressed – as he had done since the time of women's suffrage. Gilbert Murray wrote that 'he

---

* This *Last Essay*, and the *Last Poem*, are included in a miscellany of verse and prose collected and arranged by his widow, Evelyn Sharp, with an Introduction by Gilbert Murray, under the title, *Visions and Memories*, 1944.

always repudiated the charge that he was a champion of Lost Causes. On the contrary, he claimed to have a peculiar flair for the causes that were going to win.'

Reginald Reynolds, in his autobiography, *My Life and Crimes*,* recalls that it was Nevinson who invented the term, The Stage Army of the Good, for all of us who signed protest letters to newspapers, spoke at public meetings against imperialism, capitalism, war. I have forgotten, now, in what way Nevinson disappointed us over India, but Reginald says that he did – he evidently, for some reason, did not support Gandhi's campaign. 'But,' my late husband wrote, 'he hated to think of the old gang being at it again without his presence, and he had turned up at a dinner on Gandhi's birthday, in October 1930, when Gandhi was in prison; and every other guest, I am sure, was a hundred per cent pro-Gandhi in the political struggle.' Many were there whom Nevinson 'recognized as old colleagues, blessing them without quite approving of this new venture. "It's the same old crowd," he said, scowling affectionately round the room, "the people who opposed the Boer War, the people who stood up for Ireland, the people who backed Women's Suffrage and all the unpopular causes. *It's the Stage Army of the Good!*" '

H. N. Brailsford, in an Introduction to *Essays, Poems and Tales*,† which he assembled and edited after Henry Nevinson's death, says of him that 'women owe him a lasting debt, for Nevinson did more than any other man to help them in the last round of their long and bitter struggle to gain the vote', and it was not cheap service, for he 'threw up a congenial post on a Liberal newspaper and said "farewell to Fleet Street" (as one of his essays put it) in protest against its policy on this question'. He was lost and unhappy when he left Fleet Street, nostalgically recalling the bustle and excitement of the 'stuff' coming in from all over the world, the columns to be written, the ruthless cutting, the orchestration of news – 'It was a grand orchestra, that of ours. Night by night it played the symphony of the world, and each night a new symphony was performed, without rehearsal.' He visualized the leader-writer coming out into Fleet Street in the early hours, 'exhausted, but with the happy sense of

* 1956.   † 1948.

function fulfilled. . . . He is some hours in front of the
morning's news, and in a few hours more half a million
people will be reading what he has just written . . .' and there
he stood, at night, beside a suburban lamp-post, wondering
how to pass the time till bedtime – 'Think of a journalist
wanting to kill time!'

But Henry Nevinson was more than a journalist, he was,
more importantly, as H. N. Brailsford pointed out in his
preface to the selection of poems, essays and tales, a literary
craftsman. In the tales he included in his selection there is a
story, *The St George of Rochester*, reminiscent of Tomlinson in
that it is a story of London's river, and the barge men who
work on it. It is told by a dying lighterman to another man,
of whom he asks a final service. He had been captain of a
sailing barge, hailing from Rochester to the West Kent
Wharf, close by London Bridge. Then one Saturday afternoon a young woman comes down the steps of the wharf
and stands looking – 'the same as mostly stands watchin', no
matter if there ain't nothin' to watch'. He gets into conversation with her, unable to bear seeing a female standing by
herself and not speak to her, it seeming impolite, a rejection,
so he looks up at her and says, 'quite gentle' – 'Eh, miss, it's
I wish you were comin' down the water with me, I do.'
She replies that she is coming, 'and steps down the gunwale
as cool as gettin' into a penny 'bus.' The next moment they'd
swung out into the stream and down under the bridge. He
gives her tea and offers to put her ashore at Gravesend or
Rotherhithe, but she pleads with him to allow her to remain
on board and not send her back to London all alone. She will
live on the deck, she says, or wherever there's room, and do
the cooking and washing 'and look after the ship, and make
it all nice. Only don't turn me away.'

She is an attractive and refined female, and he has always
been 'terrible fond o' females' and can't bear to see them in
distress, and he allows her to stay and gives her a cabin and
asks what they shall call her. She says it doesn't matter, and
asks are they a long way from London now. He tells her
they're past Erith 'and makin' up to Purfleet'. Erith is a
pretty name, she says; they can call her that. She makes
herself useful in the ship, but keeps herself to herself. At

Christmas time she starts sewing, and at Easter she has a baby born to her in the barge – 'not a convenient kind o' place for such things to 'appen, but I brought off a doctor from Rochester'. The child is a boy and the name Lucky sticks to him. Erith adores him, 'as if he was the only one baby in the world'. After the birth of the child she changes in her attitude to the captain and they become lovers and are very happy – the captain's wife is dead and he is free and would like to marry Erith, but she wouldn't hear of it – he never knew why; she never speaks of her past and he has too much respect for her to ask. She continues to make herself useful in the barge, but if she had done nothing, he tells the man to whom he was recounting the story, he would have loved her 'just exackly the same by reason of the way she 'ad of lovin' me'.

But it was all too good to last, and one day little Lucky falls overboard and is drowned and they never recover the body, though Erith goes on searching, wading about in the mud. After a few weeks she gives up and he thinks she is resigned, but one night she wakens him in the night with her weeping, asks him if he had been happy with her, and whether he would do the same again if she asked to come aboard, and he assures her that that's 'a nonsensical kind of question' and believes that his kisses and endearments reassure her, but in the morning she is gone and he never sets eyes on her again. 'She must 'ave climbed out over the other barges and up on to the wharf, she bein' always active as a cat.' He tries to understand why she has gone, thinking perhaps that with brooding so much on the boy she got to thinking of her own people again, or perhaps the river reminded her too much of the boy and she was always seeing his ghost, on the water or in the cabin. Or maybe, he thinks, 'as soon as the child went down with the ebb, it kind o' took the daylight off everythink, and she couldn't abide no more'.

The captain marries again – it's all fifteen years ago when he tells the story – and now he is dying, and he asks the man to whom he has recounted it all if he will go every Saturday at the flood, if he can get off at the time, and look out for Erith and if ever he sees her to address her by that name and tell her ' 'ow I kep' on waiting for 'er till I'd got to go out, and when I'd got to go, I went bearin' 'er in mind.' And he is to give her his Doggett badge, which he won over thirty years ago, and which she used to make shine in their cabin. 'It 'ud bring 'er in something if needful, either melted down or sold back to the Fishmongers' Company, as gives such things.' He adds that perhaps they'd like to hear of him again, 'seein' it was a grand race the year I won it'.

The man to whom the story is told promises – but his wife, when he tells her, is caustic. Men make fools of themselves, she declares, scornfully, and wasn't that woman 'mighty glad to get somewhere to 'ave 'er child in quiet and a fine, strong man workin' to feed them both!' Then as soon as she had no more use for him she was off – and serve him right for being such a softy. Perhaps the captain was fooled, but reading his account of the romance it's impossible to believe so; what is recounted is a *love* story.

I enjoyed re-reading it very much, and having just re-read *Gallions Reach* felt that Tomlinson could have written it, but when Nevinson wrote that story I do not know, or whether he was influenced by Tomlinson. His other stories – Cockney stories – in this Brailsford selection I do not greatly care for, but I enjoyed re-reading some of the *Essays in Freedom* (1909) and the *Essays in Rebellion* (1913), and of the *Later Essays* (1936) I liked particularly his essay on religion, *The Fool's Paradise*. Nevinson, as Gilbert Murray reminds us, was 'a steady and loyal member of the Rationalist Press Association', though 'quick to admire mystics and dreamers'.

Conrad, Tomlinson, Cunninghame Graham, Henry Nevinson, I have enjoyed re-reading them all in the past few months, but there is only one I shall re-read so long as I am capable of reading at all, and that is the 'sea dreamer', Conrad.

16

Some reflections on monarchism

Despite all the re-reading I occasionally read a new book. I read the collection of Corvo pieces – some short stories and articles – put together by Cecil Woolf and published by him as *The Armed Hands, and Other Stories and Pieces*, in 1974, and I read Willie Hamilton's diatribe against the British royal family, *My Queen and I*, published in 1975. Tremendous admirer of the work of Frederick Rolfe, 'Baron Corvo', as I am, the latest addition to Corviniana proved disappointing. It is a scraping of the bottom of the barrel for any remaining fragments – eight of the pieces had not been published before – and in my view the barrel had been better left unscraped. A story entitled *Daughter of the Doge*, one of the hitherto unpublished pieces, is a kind of synopsis for what was to be what is probably Corvo's greatest work, his novel, *The Desire and Pursuit of the Whole*. The title story, *The Armed Hands*, is another hitherto unpublished work, and so far as I am concerned had better been left unpublished, for it is a silly and rather nasty story about a man with evidently a persecution mania who wore a ring with a spur mounted on it as a weapon of defence. In his introduction to the book Cecil Woolf mentions that Symons recalled that Rolfe wore such a ring 'for the purpose of protecting himself from kidnapping attempts, and he wore it in consequence of an assault on his person made years before by the Jesuits. When they essayed, as he fully expected, a further abduction, he would sweep with his armed hand at the brow of his assailant. A line would thus be scored in the flesh which would draw blood; and his blinded enemy (blinded by the dripping

blood) would be at the mercy of the intended victim.' Both
Rolfe's persecution mania where the Catholic Church was
concerned, and his pederastry, emerge very strongly in this
miscellany, and some of the writing even seems slovenly. I
had no pleasure of the book, and regard it as a very minor –
even unworthy – addition to my Corvo shelf.

From Willie Hamilton's book I derived a certain wry
satisfaction, for he has, as we say, 'done his homework' on
the subject very thoroughly, though I would have preferred
a less journalistic approach on personalities – to refer to
Princess Margaret as 'our royal, plumping princess' for
example, does not help the argument against the Monarchy,
nor does the reference to the Queen Mother 'taking a drop
of the hard stuff, her native Scotch whisky'. If Princess
Margaret is putting on weight in middle-age that is her
misfortune, but one shared by many people, along with her
mother's liking for a drop of the hard stuff. Royals are
human beings like everyone else, and the case against them
is not as persons but of their existence as part of the out-
dated monarchical system. The case is against the system,
not the people who currently compose it. Thus I would
quarrel with the jacket of the book which depicts the Queen's
head on a $3\frac{1}{2}$p stamp, with her hair straggling under her
crown, and a tear rolling down her face. What is important
is the point Willie Hamilton makes in his chapter on How
the Monarchy Survives when he says that it is a 'cornerstone
of reaction, conservatism and privilege in a world of revolution, change and challenge'.

I write as a life-long Republican. My own objection to
monarchism is the falsity of the values attached to it, the
adulation of very ordinary people, plus the enormous waste
of public money required for its upkeep. I regard it, also, as
an anachronism in the late twentieth century.

Willie Hamilton makes much – rightly, to my mind – of
the fantastic, the preposterous, cost of the upkeep of the
British royal family, and the enormous increases made in
1972 in response to the royal pay claim put in by the Queen,
'signed by Her Majesty's own hand', in 1971, and by which
her emolument – if that is the word – was more than doubled,
from £475,000 a year to £980,000, with the Queen Mother

receiving £95,000 a year – an increase of £25,000, an extra £500 a week. Princess Margaret was bumped up from £15,000 a year to £20,000. All this is, of course, tax free.

It used to be said – and I readily admit to being one of those who said it – that the British Monarchy cost the rate payers a million pounds sterling a year, but Willie Hamilton cites *The Observer*, for 5 December 1971, as pointing out that this is misleading, 'because it does not include, for instance, expenditure on the royal yacht – which is getting on for a million a year in itself, or on the maintenance of royal palaces and residences, which take another million'. The royal yacht is apparently only in use an average sixty-seven days a year. *The Observer* did not mention the royal train, which is used even less, but which costs over £33,000 a year, or the Queen's Flight, whose annual running costs are £800,000 a year. There is also the question of the Grace and Favour Residences, the taxpayers' bills for which can be, in Willie Hamilton's words, 'quite substantial'. They should all be, as he says, 'handed over to the local authority, so that they can be allocated according to genuine need'. Willie Hamilton provides many more figures concerning the cost of the upkeep of the monarchy, and it does, of course, all add up to absurdity, particularly in these inflationary times when there is so much discussion of the need to cut public expenditure. An important point is the closely guarded secret of the Queen's private fortune.

All this is extremely interesting, but since governments are addicted to squandering the taxpayers' money it is less important than the social and moral issues involved in the monarchical system, which perpetuates the class system of society, based on inherited wealth, and the power and privilege that is part of it. I am entirely with Willie Hamilton in his assertion that the monarchy and its privileges is an immoral system. It is immoral in its negation of the basic equality of Man, and in the false values it engenders. A common defence of monarchy is that it introduces 'colour', romance, pageantry, into the otherwise drab greyness of everyday life, and that the mass of people prefer a king or a queen to a president for that reason. I would personally dispute that the lives of the mass of people are drab and grey, and would suggest that they are more interesting and colourful now than, probably, at any point in history, what with colour television, package tours to foreign parts, and the prevailing sexual permissiveness. It is significant that the monarchy is now subject to open criticism. Willie Hamilton cites a *Daily Mirror* poll – 1971 – among young people about their attitude to the monarchy, 2 000 in the 15–19 age-group being interviewed, and of these 42 per cent 'thought that none of the royal family was in touch with everyday life, and an even higher proportion thought of them as *not* an ordinary family'. 'Young people,' Willie Hamilton observes, 'increasingly question the usefulness of existing institutions, especially those based on the hereditary principle.' He adds, 'Certainly the mystique of royalty is fast disappearing, killed stone dead by television.' As an example he cites the pre-wedding interview of Princess Anne and her fiancé, which revealed 'stark limitations in the Princess's intellect, vocabulary and imagination'. I have no television, but heard some of this on radio, and would entirely agree; Her Royal Highness was painfully inadequate, though the interviewers were the quintessence of tact and deference. Her young man helped her out as best he could, but he, also, made a pretty poor showing. I agree with Willie Hamilton that such revelations are healthy for the nation, as witness to 'the shortcomings of a very ordinary family for whom extraordinary claims are made by its supporters'.

Supporters of the monarchical system maintain that a monarchy gives value for money – that it is, as one strong monarchist put it to me, 'a good buy'. There has to be a head of state – so runs the argument – and a monarchy is less likely to be corrupt than a presidency which would cost as much . . . which I would think not true, for the nation does not have to support a president's entire family. Willie Hamilton regards the 'cost' argument, with the assertion that our monarchy is cheap at the price, even a profit-maker, as 'trivial and irrelevant', since 'it is impossible to make international comparisons, and equally impossible for anyone to put a price-tag on the Royals', adding that 'having said that, it is hard to see what we have left except a pleasure-giving symbol, like the neon-lights at Piccadilly Circus or a firework show, and a totem pole for tribal capitalism'.

It is commonly urged, too, that royal visits abroad are 'good for trade' and for the upholding of our national prestige; the monarch is seen as a kind of super Public Relations Officer. Is a monarch really more useful than a president in this respect? I should not have thought so; it is anyhow immeasurable.

Another argument in favour of monarchism is that a monarchy is a tourist attraction. Do England and Holland and Sweden really attract more tourists per annum than France and Italy and Spain? The evidence would not seem to be so.

But the clinching argument, always, is that a monarchy represents stability – we are all one huge happy family, headed by the Royal Family; which of course is self-evident nonsense, for monarchist countries are as deeply divided on political and social issues as presidential countries.

There have been popular monarchs in this country within our time; Edward VII, I suppose was, perhaps not so much despite as because of his goings-on; George V and Queen Mary seem to have commanded respect – perhaps even affection; Edward VIII was definitely popular – he had 'charisma' and was a break-away from royal stuffiness, and was never more popular than when the news broke of his romance with Mrs Simpson; when he went into exile in France, after his abdication, there were those who revived the Jacobean toast of 'to the king across the water'. He commanded a large measure of popular sympathy, but he nevertheless let down the royal side, and royalty have been letting it down, one way and another, ever since. Which is to the good; the more Royals behave like ordinary human beings the more manifestly absurd it is to adulate them as super-humans – and you cannot fool all the people all the time; for a long time, it is true, but not forever.

Willie Hamilton cites Tom Paine's 'Address to the People of France' on the occasion of Louis XVI's flight on 25 October 1792: 'Royalty is as repugnant to common sense as to the common right . . . of all superstitions, none has more debased men's minds.'

But there is no Republican movement in this country, and the monarchy, as Willie Hamilton admits, is unlikely to be deposed overnight. 'Britain is not a country that is easily rocked by revolution. . . . In Britain our institutions evolve. We are a Fabian Society writ large. The one thing we can be sure of is that, if the Monarchy is still with us fifty years from now, it will not be the Monarchy of the 1970s.' We are probably, almost certainly, stuck with Charles III, but that young man's own generation, coming to maturity, is, already, a great deal less romantic-sentimental about monarchism than its parents – 'less susceptible to hocus-pocus, and more realistic in its demands', as Willie Hamilton put its, and 'a third of the United Kingdom's citizens would probably vote for a republic if given the chance to do so'. And if the monarchy ceased to exist the rest would not mind all that much, recognizing that what had passed was an anachronism in a changing world.

Royalty is already a degree less popular than it was; Princess Margaret and Princess Anne are definitely un-popular, and Prince Philip's facetiousness – and often downright rudeness – does not pass with the mass of common people as wit. Even the 'pageantry' of royalty begins to seem somewhat old-hat – like the glamour that once accrued to Hollywood film stars. A common people addicted to colour television is highly sophisticated – and increasingly blasé. The popular press is increasingly disrespectful, speculating on whether Princess Anne is 'on the pill', and whether Prince Charles will be 'the first old-age pensioner to be crowned king' – and should he be. Even the *Financial Times* (3 December 1971) asks bluntly, 'How much is the Queen's private income?' Whilst *The Guardian* for 7 December referred to the Royal Family as 'the Head of the Establishment and the font of so much British snobbism, mumbo-jumbo and traditionalist complacency'.

We have come a long way since Leigh Hunt was sent to prison for two years, on 13 February 1813, for writing in his weekly paper *The Examiner* that, contrary to what the *Morning Post* had written on the occasion of the Regent's fiftieth birthday, the Prince was no Adonis but a 'corpulent man of fifty', and, moreover, 'a violator of his word, a libertine over head and ears in disgrace, a despiser of domestic ties, and the companion of gamblers and demireps'. His brother, co-founder of the paper, was also sent to prison for two years; the brothers were in separate prisons, and each had to pay a fine of £500. Young Shelley sent Leigh Hunt £20 towards the fine, and a juror with a guilty conscience offered him £500, which he refused, though he borrowed – not from the juror – several hundred pounds to transform his two prison rooms into a comfortable and tasteful apartment, furnished with bookcases and a piano, into which he moved his wife and children, and in which he received many distinguished literary guests, including Tom Moore, Byron, William Hazlitt, Charles and Mary Lamb, and Keats's painter friend, Benjamin Haydon. He continued to edit *The Examiner* and write political commentary for it, and Thomas Barnes of *The Times*, another of his prison visitors, and Hazlitt, both became regular contributors. Cowden Clarke, Keats's great friend and one-time tutor, visited Hunt in prison every week and joined in the literary discussions – and *The Examiner* flourished. As Keats's biographer, Dr Aileen Ward, observes, 'Imprisonment made Hunt's name as a martyr to the liberal cause.' When Hunt was released, on 2 February 1815, Keats commemorated the occasion with a sonnet which he gave Cowden Clarke to pass to Hunt – which was the first Cowden Clarke knew of Keats writing poetry – and thereby committed himself to Hunt's fearless liberalism. He was to become Hunt's literary protégé, and Hunt his great friend.

George IV, both as Regent and King, was thoroughly unadmirable, all that Leigh Hunt declared him to be, and his successor, William IV, did little or nothing to overcome popular disgust with the Hanoverian monarchy, yet still there was no stirring of any Republicanism, and England moved on to the long, patriotic devotion to Queen Victoria. She had her period of unpopularity, after Albert's death, when she became the secluded 'widow of Windsor', but, nevertheless, she died revered, and the Monarchy as firmly entrenched as ever.

But all that is another world, another life. In the late twentieth century the stream of life moves fast, and the generation reaching maturity today is already far ahead of the previous generation and sweeps along with a massive contempt for the Establishment in all its forms. The Monarchy like the Church, has little chance of survivial. Institutions have their day – often a very long day, but are eventually 'dumped in the garbage can of history', as Willie Hamilton put it, and I share his belief that the end of the century will see the end of the British Monarchy. I would think, even, the end of all European monarchy. Probably also of the Hashemite Kingdom of Jordan, which was essentially a British creation.

I have respect for King Hussein of Jordan. I have had the privilege of informal talks with him in Amman and London, and have no doubt at all about his sincerity. Even in the early sixties when he was at loggerheads with President Nasser – whom I greatly admired – I maintained to indignant Arabs in Jordan that he was sincere according to his lights; they were not my lights, or those of the Palestinians, or of many Jordanians, but Hussein had his own Hashemite concept of his role as monarch, never doubting that it was right. Later he made his peace with Nasser, and then even the Palestinians ceased to write 'Down with Hussein!' on the rocks on the road up from Amman to Jerusalem. One used the expression to me, 'He's a good boy now!' He was finished for the Palestinians in 1967, following the defeat in the June War; relations with the various Palestinian groups based in Jordan deteriorated, and by 1970 it looked as though the Palestinians were setting up a state within a state; the Hashemite throne, always shaky, was seriously threatened. After the Dawson's Field jet airliner hijackings, at the end of which the Palestinian commandos blew up three 'planes, Hussein clamped down and turned his army on to the guerillas. There was something like civil war, and to the Palestinians, in what has come to be known as Black September, he became the Butcher of Amman. My sympathies are with the Palestinians, but in all this Hussein acted to protect his Kingdom – the 'hashed-up Kingdom,' I often heard it called in Amman, Damascus, and Cairo. There have been several attempts on Hussein's life, and if he finally succumbs to a Palestinian bullet, like his grandfather, Jordan is more likely than not to become a republic – as Iraq did after Faisal was murdered in the 1957 coup and General Abdel Karim Qassim took over as Head of State – himself to be murdered in a coup in 1963.

Significantly, King Hussein entitled his autobiography, published in 1962, *Uneasy Lies the Head*. In it he published a photograph of his son, by his English wife, Princess Muna – whom he has since divorced to marry a Palestinian girl – whom he named Abdullah, captioning the picture, 'My son and heir'. Personally I do not think this Anglo-Arab prince will come to the throne – a view shared by many other people who know the Arab scene. Part of the wind of change for the Palestinians, of which I have already written, is the revolutionary spirit bound up with the Resistance Movement. It was never the intention of the Palestinians to liberate Palestine from the Zionists only for it to become part of the Hashemite Kingdom; they always envisaged a Palestinian republic – socialist at that. After the Rabat conference in October 1974, when Yasser Arafat and not King Hussein was held to represent the Palestinian people, Hussein was obliged to cede his sovereignty in the West Bank – in the event of it ceasing to be Israeli Occupied Territory – to the Palestine Liberation Organization. He thus now only rules over the truncated remains of the Hashemite Kingdom, the East Bank – the erstwhile Trans-Jordan.

King Hussein had survived a great deal, but whilst he physically might survive the re-establishment of Palestine as an Arab country, it is problematic as to whether his kingship would. To be sure, the *bedu*, who compose his army, are passionately loyal to him, but I wonder about the civilian population, a considerable part of which is Palestinian. The monarchy could be swept away in the revolutionizing wind of change.

Unlike our own monarchy, which will go out with neither a bang nor a whimper, but just be, politely, bowed out – in the evolutionary British manner. By the end of this fast-moving century.

It is perhaps of some interest that in the summer of 1974 I was invited – to my very great astonishment – to a Royal

Garden Party, or, as the Lord Chamberlain's invitation puts it, 'to an Afternoon Party in the Garden of Buckingham Palace'. My first reaction was one of affront; my views were surely well enough known? But evidently they weren't – anyhow not to the Lord Chamberlain, whoever he may be, who declared himself 'commanded by Her Majesty' to invite me. I wouldn't, of course, go; wouldn't dream of it. Naturally. But when my indignation had worn off I thought that perhaps it might be interesting, if only to see who of the so-called Labour Left might be there. Interesting, too, to see the grounds of Buck Pal. But then the question arose, would I have to wear a hat? In common with most women nowadays – I suppose – I do not possess a hat. I made inquiries and the consensus of opinion was that a hat would be called for. I went as far as looking vaguely around the millinery department of the local stores (I was then, of course, living in London) and even tried on a few hats . . . and decided I looked ridiculous in them. And did I, anyhow, really want to go to this huge tea-party at which I would probably know no one? Even as an 'experience' wouldn't it be, really, rather dull? There was this to be considered, too, that if I went 'out of curiosity' who was going to believe that? 'So much for her anti-monarchism!' they'd say. And they'd have a right to say it.

I don't know whether it was that which settled it for me, or the hat business, or the feeling that it would be a bore. Anyhow I returned the invitation to the Lord Chamberlain, as required in the event of non-usage. No disrespect to Her Majesty; it was very nice of her to invite me – especially as she has never heard of me . . . plus the fact that these garden parties must be very boring indeed for her.

I have not received any subsequent invitation. If ever I do – which I think unlikely – I shall again tender the Lord Chamberlain my 'regrets'.

17

Some reflections on old age

In my last volume of autobiography, *Stories from my Life*, published in 1973, I devoted three chapters to the subject of old age, entitling them, 'Three-Score-Years-and-Ten', 'The Quiet Rhythm', and 'At Close of Play'. When I wrote those chapters I had three-score-years-and-twelve; now it is fifteen, and when you are old three years makes a difference – every year makes a difference, for there is the steady diminution of mental and physical energy. When I wrote *Stories from my Life* in 1972 I was sure that I had made my last overseas journey, but, as it turned out, I had my seventy-third birthday in Venice, having set out – by boat and train – in the autumn of 1973 for northern Italy to gather material for a book to be called *An Italian Journey*. The book was published in December 1974, and settled now in Devon, between the high moor and the sea, it is unlikely I shall ever make another journey or write another travel book. There was some talk of my making a second Italian journey and covering southern Italy, but I could not face the physical wear and tear of such a journey, nor the loneliness – for these solo journeys can be desperately lonely, journeying alone, wandering about alone, eating alone, drinking alone, and never anyone with whom to relax at the end of the day. Already the nearing-seventy-three I was then seems remote from the nearing-seventy-five I am now; as I have said, once launched into the seventies every year counts.

Make no mistake about it – once you have passed the three-score-and-ten mark you are old, and you had better accept the fact. There will always be people to assure you that you 'don't look it', and they say it to be kind, to be reassuring, or to flatter, or out of politeness, and perhaps one in ten is sincere and really means it, really does think you don't look or seem your age, but whether you do or not the physical fact of your age relentlessly remains, taking its toll of energy and vitality. Certainly there are people who at seventy-odd look no more than sixty-five, but whatever one *looks* like it is a biological fact that between the sixties and seventies the difference in terms of physical energy, nervous capacity, and mental drive is enormous. Those still the vigorous sunny side of seventy will query this, but those who have passed the seventy landmark will agree; they know.

It was all very well for Somerset Maugham to write in his autobiographical book, *The Summing Up*, published in 1938 that he looked forward to old age without dismay – he was sixty-four at the time and hadn't got there; he could then envisage the 'compensations' of old age, in terms of liberation from the 'trammels of human egoism', and of sex. Twenty years later, in his last book, *Points of View*, published in 1958, he declared, writing of Goethe, that 'what makes old age hard to bear is not the failing of one's faculties, mental and physical, but the burden of one's memories'. That may have been true for him, but I do not believe it is true for most people. It is certainly not true for me. For me what makes old age hard to bear is that life has lost its savour, and truly if the salt hath lost its savour wherewith shall it be salted? There is no zest to life any more; nothing is exciting, and anything out of the daily routine – such as seeing people outside of the intimate circle – is a physical and nervous effort. Outside of the near-and-dear, people matter less and less; one can't-be-bothered. One is no longer amused, or for that matter much interested; all one wants is the quiet life, with no demands made, no efforts called for. To correspond is easier than to entertain, and, speaking for myself, still gives one pleasure. It is pleasant, and stimulating, to receive a lively letter, and pleasant to reply to it; and more can get said in an averagely long letter than in a whole afternoon or evening of conversation – and without the nervous exhaustion. Letters are a life-line; there is no need to *see* people – the important thing is to keep in touch, and correspondence serves this purpose admirably, and without the nervous strain and effort involved in meeting. I have a number of old friends whom I am unlikely ever to meet again, but that is all right, so long as they write – maintain the life-line. In youth it is always 'lovely to see you!' in old age seeing people involves a physical and mental effort, and can be – and very often is – nervously exhausting. I have friends whom I have never met; it is not necessary that we should meet; nothing would be gained by it – there might even be a mutual loss.

When life loses its savour, as it does with the descent into the seventies, it becomes somewhat boring. To be sure the cherry-blossom is as beautiful every spring, and one is aware of it, and of the apple-blossom and lilac that follow, and the first June roses, but it is not the excitement, the lyric ecstasy, it once was. There is even a little sadness in it, with the speculation as to how many more times you will see it all. A certain melancholy is inseparable from old age for probably most people, I think. According to Michael Holroyd's biography, Augustus John, after his rich and full youth and middle age, suffered much from old age melancholia, and took to drink to escape from the inner emptiness.

Not long ago I wrote to a distinguished woman novelist, now in her eighties and no longer writing, and asked her whether she was as bored in old age as I was. She replied, 'Bored? Indescribably, abysmally, icily!' I am not, myself, as bored as that, for despite mental and physical inertia I maintain a few interests: I am interested in the book I am currently writing – though writing is a hard slog nowadays; and I am interested in the garden I re-made when I came here – though lack the physical energy to do as much in it as I'd like to; I remain interested in the Middle East, though except for the occasional article am no longer active in the Palestine struggle; I enjoy letters from friends, though outside of the intimate circle it is an effort to see people. The days when there are no letters, or when the mail is uninteresting, are somewhat 'dead' days, for when you cease to go anywhere except to the local shops and see very few people, you tend to 'live' in the mail as contact with the outside world. For me there is nothing more deadly than bank holidays, when sometimes for days on end there is neither mail nor newspaper – but this is not an old age thing; I have always felt it. I suppose the greatest modern escape from boredom, for young and old alike, is television, but I dislike it as a medium, and so long as there are letters and *The Times* at breakfast time I can 'get by'.

There are, of course, people who are 'wonderful' in old age, and I think they really *are* wonderful, charging about in 'planes from country to country, apparently tirelessly, flying the Atlantic and giving press interviews the moment they step out on to the tarmac, unaffected, it would seem, by mental and physical exhaustion and the time lag; not to mention people in their seventies and eighties who think nothing of flying to Australia to visit members of their families. It is remarkable, and it is admirable, but it is not the norm. I hear and read of authors who go on writing novels in their eighties, and am awed – as one always is by something quite beyond one's own capability. I wrote a novel* when I was seventy-four; I wrote it fairly quickly, but I expect – and hope – it will be my last. I do not think I any longer have the mental and nervous strength required for the sustained creative effort that writing a novel is. I recall some years ago reading that Simenon would write no more of his thrillers, no longer, he said, having the 'strength'. I was only in my sixties, then, but I knew what he meant.

The waning of energy, mental and physical, is a curse of old age, with all that it involves of frustration, but it is a disadvantage that can also be turned to advantage, in that it absolves you from making those efforts which are so hard to make. A friend of mine looked forward to being seventy so that he could give way to feeling old without feeling guilty about it – he having felt old already for some years past. This surrender to lack of energy is a negative compensation of old age; on the positive side there is the ending of self-consciousness, no longer caring what people think, so that you can wear what you like, say what you like, do what you like – giving yourself dispensations for not doing what you don't want to do, for getting out of things, and for allowing yourself that extra drink, that snooze in the afternoon.

* *The Late Miss Guthrie,* 1976.

Jean Rhys, writing on old age in *The Times* (21 May 1975) mentioned as one of the compensations the fact that few things really matter any more. 'This indifference, or calm, or whatever you like to call it,' she wrote, 'is like a cave at the back of your mind, where you can retire and be alone and safe.' But she also wrote of knowing that there would 'never again be a day when you felt really well'. For myself I would qualify that never, though with more days than not of not-feeling-really-well I know what she means; luckier than she is I do have the occasional days of feeling well, and they come as a bonus. People vary tremendously, of course, and there are people in their eighties whose general health and vigour is good, and who are not subject to good and bad days. They are to be envied, but are, I think, the exceptions.

Maugham said the old age was all right so long as you had health and money. Certainly to be old and poor and ill is grim, especially if the misery is compounded with loneliness. Health is very much a concern of old age; there is always the background dread of a stroke, or a fall, of being carted, helplessly, off to hospital. For the lucky ones – and there are plenty of them – it doesn't happen, and they 'go gently into that last goodnight', dying suddenly, or in their sleep, or at worst after only brief illnesses.

I do not, myself, reflect very much on all this, but I do reflect on two things which I regard as very important – the case for voluntary euthanasia, and the case for not telling patients with terminal illnesses that they have only a few more weeks to live. Doctors are admired for their honesty when they tell their patients the stark truth, but such honesty destroys hope, and without hope we cannot live. What is the point of administering the brutal truth, of issuing a death sentence, when the more human thing would be to be less honest and hold out a little hope, even if falsely? Usually the doctor who issues a death sentence is right, but he *could* be wrong, and it ought to be a medical principle that whilst there's life there's hope. I have seen more than once someone sentenced to death by the doctor give up the struggle, whereas a gleam of hope might have prolonged life. It might not have, but also it might, and doctors should surely give their patients a chance, and hope, however slight, is always a life-line.

Bracketed in importance with this is the question of voluntary euthanasia, and it is one which by no means concerns only the old but all adult human beings, since at any age there may develop the kind of illness which makes life intolerable and a merciful release from it to be preferred. There is a great deal of misunderstanding concerning voluntary euthanasia, in connection with which the key word is *voluntary*. It is not an arbitrary putting-down of the old and sick, but a compact entered into between patient and doctor by which the doctor agrees to carry out the patient's wish for termination when suffering becomes too much or the continuation of life only on unacceptable terms.

In the words of the Voluntary Euthanasia Society, of which I have long been a member, the plea for legislation to permit voluntary euthanasia 'would give to an adult, in carefully defined circumstances and with proper safeguards, the choice between prolonged suffering and gentle, dignified death'. It cannot be too strongly stressed that Voluntary Euthanasia is *not* 'mercy killing', in which someone, for compassionate reasons, decides to take the life of another. It is a fundamental principle of the Society's policy that euthanasia would be administered *only* at the expressed wish of the individual, and then only in carefully defined circumstances and with all possible safeguards against abuse. The Society does not advocate the putting down of the old and infirm, or of deformed and mentally defective children. Voluntary euthanasia at the hands of a sympathetic and understanding doctor is for those for whom suffering which drugs cannot alleviate has become intolerable.

Every human being has the right to live, and equally the right to die. This I do most profoundly believe. There are circumstances in which we speak of death as a 'merciful release', but that release is often protracted, even, by medical science, postponed; voluntary euthanasia gives the patient the right to opt out when the situation becomes intolerable, and it should be legal for the doctor, at the patient's request, to assist this termination. Some doctors do, of course, enter into this compact – we shall never know how many, but in a rational society it would be possible for them to stand up and be counted. It will come, and the time is probably not far ahead, in spite of all the objections of the churchmen, the prejudiced, and the ignorant. I would personally like to see legalized the putting down – at the request of the parents – of children born grossly malformed and mentally defective, but though society has made big strides towards rationality in the last few decades it has still a long way to go.

I reflect a good deal on the problems of retirement, this being very much a retirement village. During the holiday months of July and August there are a great many young people, including children, but when that high tide of visitors has ebbed it is to be seen that the majority of people left behind are elderly. They have in their time come here as summer visitors, from the Midlands, the North, London, and, charmed, have settled on it for their retirement, their dream bungalow in Devonshire – what could be nicer? And in this Teignmouth–Shaldon area it is, of course, very nice, with the combination of sea and country, and 'bus services to Torquay one way and Exeter the other, so that there is no feeling of being cut off.

Then, in due course, the much-looked-forward-to retirement becomes a reality, and with luck the Devon bungalow or small house is found, the dream comes true, and the move from Birmingham or London or wherever is effected. The sea-and-country landscape measures up to the dream; the weather is milder, and the daylight longer, than in Birmingham or London; the local people are friendly; it is pleasant to walk along the estuary to the small village shops, or to get the 'bus over the bridge into quiet little Teignmouth for the bigger ones. The air is clean and good; there is no pollution, and no jet 'planes scream over. No one in their senses would wish to be back in London or Birmingham. Of course not. And no one is bored – what an idea! But the fact remains that in London and Birmingham or wherever the man had a job; he had a regular routine, which in turn ordered the woman's routine; now from the time he gets up to the time he goes to bed the man has nothing to do; the woman's routine of shopping, meal-getting, housework remains, though no longer geared to the man's absence during the day and his return home in the evening. Now instead of an evening meal she gets a mid-day one – and he is there all the time . . . inescapably. Well, but perhaps he plays golf, and that takes him out of the house for the better part of a day, but then she is lonely as she never was in London or Birmingham when he was simply away at the office. She could never resent him going off to the office; it was essential he should do so; but when he takes a day off to play golf, leaving her alone, she is resentful. In the old life she had the busyness of town life to distract her; here in the rural setting she feels she has nothing, and she is bored; the man, too, is bored, except when he is at the golf club or, perhaps, at the local. He gardens, keeping the lawn immaculate; he always gardened at the weekends in the old life, and enjoyed it, but now it is almost a full-time occupation, for what else is there to do? You can go for walks, to be sure, but it is not long before the walk along the estuary and down to the beach and round and back through the village – which is about the only walk there is – becomes as boring as the daily walk to the station in the old suburban days. For her the novelty of the village shops soon wears off, and neither the over-sixties club nor the weekly sewing-class appeal to her – indeed, in the old life she would have ridiculed both.

So there they are, living in this pleasant place, in the dream bungalow, and suffering the boredom of retirement. If they had not retired to the country it would have been easier for them. They were betrayed by a romantic dream. In town they would have been sustained by the bustle and activity all about them; in the rural setting the quietness they had sought becomes a trap, enclosing them, and unless you are village-minded, and interested in jumble sales and coffee mornings and church functions, there is literally nothing to do – except work in the garden, and some days it is too cold for that, or too hot, or too windy, or one just isn't in the mood.

This is the great problem of retirement – how to avoid boredom. In the short time I have been here, some eighteen months as I write, I have seen this problem in all its insolubility. One woman busies herself in village affairs; the man potters in the garden, and reads. I don't know whether he is bored; she certainly isn't – she has no time to be. But another woman is a golf-widow, and with a charming bungalow and garden yearns for a flat in Torquay – for good shops, and cafés, and a bit of life; and who shall blame her? She lacks the temperament for involvement in the village life; she does not drive a car, and, alone a great deal, her days are empty. He has the life at the golf club, with 'the chaps'; she has nothing. In the town from which she came she could at least have gone to the cinema sometimes in the afternoons, or gone window-shopping, and there would have been the feeling of life in the busy streets; here there is only the silence, broken by the occasional fretful cry of gulls.

The widows seem to do better; they came here originally with their husbands for retirement, but have learned to adapt themselves to being alone – even learned to like it. Or they came in their widowhood to be near a married son or daughter, and they readily adapted. If boredom set in with their husbands' retirement it is something they have long outlived.

I was interested in a profile of George Woodcock – who resigned as General Secretary of the T.U.C. in 1969 and became the first chairman of the Commission on Industrial Relations – in *The Times* (9 June 1975) in which at the end of a long discourse on the economic situation in this country he gave 'a sudden great laugh', his interviewer, Brian Connell reports, 'as he thinks of the impotence of retirement at his house in Epsom', and how he does gardening 'under duress' – the rough work, because he is not a skilled gardener and doesn't like gardening anyway, regarding it as a futile exercise – 'You mow the lawn one day and three days later you need to mow it again, there's no end to it', and how he spends his time 'taking things easy', adding, 'I find retirement terribly corrupting, at least to a fellow like me. I suppose I am like the T.U.C. – I react. I can always decide that I'll start tomorrow and not bother about doing it today. I don't get up too early. I have my coffee and I've got to do my cross-word and then it's lunchtime. I do my two, three or four letters. Then I think well, "I'll have a cup of tea now," and then I think the television news will be on in half an hour.'

Undoubtedly television provides great relief from boredom – for the boredom of teenagers, the ultimate boredom of married life, and above all, I think, for the boredom of retirement. How people coped with retirement before the advent of television is difficult to imagine in this age when the majority of people have it; but then retirement was not always the problem it is now; people did not necessarily retire in their sixties, or at all; many people, indeed, took pride in the idea of 'dying in harness'. My father retired from the G.P.O. at the age of sixty after forty years as a sorter, and retirement presented no problem for him, for the simple reason that, as he would admit, he was good at doing nothing, and he had fifteen years of it – and told me on his death bed that those years had been 'sweet'. In 1933, when he retired, it was the era of the wind-up gramophone and you did not necessarily have 'the wireless'. My father spent his retirement reading and doing nothing. He occasionally, like George Woodcock, did a bit of gardening 'under duress', but his heart was not in it. His method, when required to plant something, was to dig a hole and shove the plant in and then command it, impatiently, 'Now grow, damn you, grow!' In fine weather he would sit on a bench at the bottom of the garden – beyond reach of his wife's nagging – and, as he liked to say, sometimes he would sit and think and at other times just sit.

Well, with the Irish in him, he was blessed with that temperament. Unlike my mother, who kept herself busy in house and garden right up to the day of her sudden death at the age of eighty-five. She read a great deal, listened to radio, and firmly resisted television. She could not, she declared, 'be bothered with it'. I had more in common with my father than with my mother, but I did not inherit his gift for enjoying complete idleness.

I garden, nowadays, not because I really enjoy it – as once – but because I intensely dislike untidiness, and if you do not work in a garden it quickly becomes untidy, and therefore to my mind, unsightly. I do not enjoy weeding and hoeing, but I derive great satisfaction from the sight of a well-hoed flower-bed or border; mowing is a chore, but a mown lawn is a thing of beauty, and thus pushing a mower around becomes a creative effort. I detest planting bulbs, a tedious task, but come the spring I am always glad I endured the autumn ritual. Here in Devon I garden neither more nor less than at Oak Cottage; here as there the garden is too big for me, but I will work in its so long as I have the physical strength simply because an unkempt garden is an ugly thing, God wot!

I am surrounded here, on my brow of the hill, by beautifully kept gardens, devotedly tended by elderly people none of whom are native Devonians, but people from all over who came here for their retirement. When they are not gardening they walk their dogs – to the great detriment of the lanes – and watch television. They have worked out a retirement pattern, a *modus vivendi*, insulated against boredom – anyhow probably for most of them – and good luck to them, but television, I am sure, is a major part of the escape.

Time was, of course, when people had hobbies – amateur photography, stamp-collecting, bee-keeping; they made wool rugs, played the piano, sang in choirs; these activities still go on, to be sure; but a hobby is only a hobby, when all's said and done, it is not life-fulfilling, and modern Man needs that something more that is available to him; he needs television because it is there. Some of us do not feel this need, but we are the minority, and we need not preen ourselves on any intellectual superiority; we have other means – not necessarily better – of escaping boredom; some go a good deal to concerts and the theatre; others busy themselves in local affairs – such as tenants' associations – and social work; some, such as myself, read a great deal, listen to radio, garden, entertain, write letters, walk along the water. Activity is all, and the only antidote to boredom – at any age.

F

18

Some reflections on the contemporary scene

It is a most beautiful early June evening as I write; at nine-thirty the sun has gone down behind Dartmoor but there is still crimson in the western sky and it is reflected in the shallow low-tide water of the estuary. I have several times gone out on to the balcony and regarded the sky and the water and listened to the silence. A late blackbird hops about in the grass of the orchard below. The gulls have all disappeared to wherever it is they roost.

Then suddenly there is a blast on a horn and the roar of an engine as a motor-cycle scorches up the lane. Reflecting that we can never entirely escape the aggressive ugliness of the world we inhabit I leave the balcony, switch on a desk lamp, close the curtains against the lingering sunset, and seat myself at the typewriter. It is as good a time as any to reflect on the contemporary scene.

But, indeed, I have already had some reflections on it, reading in *The Times* twelve hours earlier that the prostitutes of Marseilles and Nice have joined their Lyons sisters in a church sit-in, 'withdrawing their labour' for the weekend, as a protest against the police. I read, also, that the N.U.R. is determined to go ahead with its strike, which will involve not only railway workers but will make life difficult and uncomfortable and frustrating for everyone . . . including those of us who have retired from the mass scene.* Locally we are threatened by a municipal workers' strike which if it comes to pass will cut off our water supplies and our sewerage

* Mercifully it was called off.

arrangements. Who was it said 'Your world, and welcome to it!'? But there's no opting out; so long as we are alive in this world we are inescapably part of it, subject to its strains and stresses, and warding off as best we can the impact of its brutality.

We live in an age of dehumanized sex, and of violence at all levels, social, political, sexual, personal. For the young it may be challenging and exciting; for the old it is depressing and alarming. We have lived through two world wars, and the cruelly – and unnecessarily – protracted Vietnam war, and another war affecting this country is not likely to come during the years that remain to us, yet violence rages all round us, with hi-jackings and kidnappings in all parts of the world, and the seemingly endless sectarian murders of Northern Ireland.

There is also that other violence, the mindless violence of football fans, of muggings and other forms of robbery with violence; and the ever-present violence present for entertainment in the cinema and on the television screen, and in novels. How much this fictionized violence contributes to the real-life violence of the streets is debatable, though I would think myself that it does contribute, for you cannot feed the young a diet of violence from their most formative years and expect them to grow up other than aggressive. The small schoolboys of my time used to play Cowboys and Injuns, brandish toy pistols and go bang-bang-you're-dead – and the Injuns it was who died; that was bad enough, but children of the same age today set up barricades and rattle away with imitation machine-guns – as I have seen even here in a Devon village. And why not, when it's all a commonplace of television – that most insidious and pernicious of influences on the young.

Compound violence with sex-for-its-own-sake and you get something very destructive indeed – socially, morally, spiritually – not only for youth but for the whole of society. When I was young-in-the-twenties there was a social and moral revolution in progress; women were cutting off their hair and moving forward into a man's world with the demand not only for equality where jobs were concerned but for equal moral and sexual freedom. We talked, then, of the 'emancipation of women', and freedom was all our cry. It produced a good deal of sexual promiscuity, to be sure, but it was relatively an age of innocence, romantic, sentimental, and unashamed of the word *love* – a word which has been replaced, largely, nowadays, by the harsh crudity of *sex*. The present generation of youth can be said to be more honest, but when it rejects love in its sexual relations it deprives itself of a basic and valuable human experience. Dehumanize sex, reduce it to the purely animal level of physical urge, and what should be a deeply emotional satisfaction becomes of no more importance that eating and defecating, on the same biological level.

Back in the 'twenties and 'thirties those of us who were the young progressives of the period felt it a point of honour to have read the last chapter of James Joyce's *Ulysses* (few, I think, can honestly claim to have read the whole work) and D. H. Lawrence's *Lady Chatterley's Lover* and, strenuously, to defend these works from the charge of obscenity levied against them . . . pornography was not, then, a word in general usage, though in 1929 there was Lawrence's little booklet, *Pornography and Obscenity*, tremendously and excitingly *avant-garde*, then, but tame stuff today. In 1929 Lawrence could write, 'What is pornography to one man is the laughter of genius to another.' But Lawrence was concerned with the so-called obscene words which got him into trouble over *Lady Chatterley*, but which are today in common usage in novels, including those of some of the most esteemed writers. I have never resorted to them myself, and it's too late in the day to start now – it's not my world, not my 'scene'. When my first volume of autobiography, *Confessions and Impressions*, was published in 1930 it was considered very shocking, though it contained no fornicatory words and was merely an expression of a modern-minded young woman's attitude to life; it advocated what we should now call the liberation of women, particularly in relation to sex and marriage, and freedom in education along the lines of A. S. Neill. It was heady stuff then, as were Neill's ideas, but it has been overtaken by a sex revolution more extreme than anything envisaged by the most radical thinkers of the twenties and thirties, and the freedom for the child which

Neill and Bertrand Russell and Homer Lane, – and a handful of others – so strenuously preached the modern child takes for granted – even to the extent of physically assaulting his teachers, apparently.

The 'sex explosion', which became the pornography explosion, really began with the Penguin publication of *Lady Chatterley* in 1961. That opened the flood-gates; after that all was permissible in print, and the so-called four-letter words became the literary fashion. Kenneth Tynan stepped into the ring with the declaration that the sex act should be shown on the stage, and that it should be the real thing if the actors were up to it. The sex revolution was on; it got off to a flying start and has never looked back; novels became more and more sexually explicit, both as to hetero- and homo-sexual relationships; a novel whose theme was masturbation rapidly became a bestseller, and sodomy was common literary coin. There was an Italian film about a young man who had a sexual passion for pigs; there was a play in which young hooligans rolled a baby in its pram in its excrement and then stoned it to death. There might have been – must surely have been – some private revulsion, but the critics applauded the play as art, and once the seal of 'art' is set upon it, any obscenity and any indecency becomes culturally acceptable in the – quite chronically – sexually liberated West.

Thus the sodomy episode in *Last Tango in Paris*, and news and particulars of a film about oral sex, occasioned a certain curiosity, and, inevitably, box-office queues; the films were seriously reviewed, and there was no popular protest. In the matter of pornography we have, it would seem, reached the point of no return, and the sexually explicit revue, *Oh, Calcutta!*, looks like running forever – and why not, since pornography, on the stage and in the cinema and in sleazy establishments whose sole *raison d'être* it is, is big business.*

* It is interesting that the nineteenth-century traveller and explorer, Sir Richard Burton, made more money out of his translation of *The Thousand and One Nights* than out of all his books and expeditions, and his wife recorded in her biography of him, published in 1893, that he declared, bitterly, 'I have struggled for forty-seven years, distinguished myself honourably in every way that I could. I translate a doubtful book in my old age, and immediately make sixteen thousand guineas. Now that I know the tastes of England, we need never be without money.'

Any form of censorship is, of course, subject to abuse, and the *Sunday Times*, 21 December 1975, cites examples of police seizing magazines even though the Director of Public Prosecutions has ruled that they are not obscene, and points out that this 'back door censorship' is contrary to the Obscene Publications Act of 1964, and produces the anomaly of publications regarded (for example) as decent in Middlesbrough seized as obscene in Newcastle. This, however, only calls for greater vigilance on the part of the D.P.P. and a stricter insistence on the law. I always agreed with D. H. Lawrence that pornography was an insult to sex, to the human body, to a vital human relationship; but I parted company with him when he declared that he would 'censor genuine pornography, rigorously'. I took, in fact, mastering instinctive reactions of horror, the correct 'liberal' line. I modified my views in the light of recent cases of violence and sexual depravity, and notably the horrible revelations in the Cambridge rapist case, in which it was disclosed that the perpetrators of these crimes had been influenced by some book or film – the Cambridge rapist was found to have been a frequent customer for porn at the local 'sex shop'. The shop, I have since read, has been ordered to be closed down, and surely it would be a good thing, sociologically, if all such dispensers of porn were – no matter what the Danes might think of us?

It is illegal to possess hard drugs, and society, in general, accepts the rightness of this attempt to control this danger; surely it makes as much sense to attempt to control the psychological evil of pornography? This, in practice, means some kind, or degree, of censorship of books, films – in the cinema and on television – stage productions, and the prohibitions of porn magazines and 'sex shops'. Censorship, I admit, is a word to shrink from, since it infringes personal freedom, to which, in a democracy, so much importance is attached; but there comes a point at which discipline is of greater value, for society and the individual, than complete liberty. We do not allow drug addicts the liberty to destroy themselves; we try to prevent it; why should not a civilized society try to prevent *moral* corruption? The defenders of pornography, of course, insist that it does not corrupt – that 'it does no harm'. But how do they know it does no harm? They have only to read their newspapers, with some attention to the police court news, to see that it does, in fact, do harm. They should also ask themselves what harm it does to *them* – whether there is not, in fact, a pollution of the mind? What we see, hear, read, if it makes any impression on us stays in the mind, and the pornographic stays strongly in the mind because of its sexuality – something fundamental to all of us. I do not *wish* to remember the pornographic excerpts from contemporary fiction which I read, from time to time, in reviews, but they stick – as the rhymes of a lewd limerick stick more readily than the lines of a beautiful poem; and because they are brutish, ugly, depraved, my mind would be better without them – as would any mind. Thus, surely, it would be better that some books were not published – at least unexpurgated – and some films and plays not produced? It is anyhow the conclusion to which I have – belatedly and reluctantly come. If this makes me a 'puritan', so be it. The term is not necessarily derogatory.

But as David Holbrook says in his courageous – and valuable book, *The Pseudo-Revolution; a Critical Study of Extremist 'Liberation' in Sex,** the 'progressives' who defend pornography 'have devised a tone which implies by its confident arrogance that all opposition is disreputable, reactionary, ill-informed, or ridiculous', and he adds, 'Most of those who feel that something is wrong fail to express their disquiet by forceful exposition, because they fear ridicule by the "sophisticated" – who can, in fact, during the present wave, always point to something more outrageous than that to which the objector is pointing. In other words, as fanatical demoralization proceeds it rapidly moves "beyond the access of moral debate".'

This late-twentieth-century upsurge of pornography and violence is the final decadence of a civilization in decline. What we are witnessing and living through are the death-throes of a civilization.

Sir John Bagot Glubb (Glubb Pasha), in one of his books about the rise and fall of the Arab Empires, *The Course of*

* 1972. Tom Stacey, Ltd.,

Empire,* noted in his preface that 'the words in which Arab historians deplore the materialism, the sexual laxity and the indifference to religion of the post-imperial period might have been written in London today', and also that 'Roman rule in Western Europe collapsed in the fourth and fifth centuries and was succeeded by six centuries of barbarism'. He notes that 'the period between Rome and the emergence of modern Europe was the same, six hundred years, as between the Arabs and the Ottomans', so that, broadly, a picture begins to emerge. Certainly there emerges in this present time the picture of Western civilization in the process of destroying itself through the acceleration of materialism in all its forms – sociological, political, personal, sexual. We can but believe – or at least hope – that a new civilization, with a new ethos, will replace the outworn old, and that the new will be a renaissance of the beautiful and the good.

To live to see and experience such a spiritual and cultural renaissance would be exhilarating, but it will hardly come this century, and in the meantime we are stuck with the decadence and self-destruction, the pornography and the violence. A generation is growing up into this world in which 'anything goes' – as we used to say in the 'sixties – but is it too much to hope that some of them – even many of them – will react against the nihilism of a society in which there are no values but the material ones, and no ideals? The young are still the hope for the future, despite the other picture, which is of youthful drug addiction, increased juvenile delinquency – particularly in the field of violence – venereal disease, and school-girl pregnancies. With the fearful pressures imposed on the young through the unremitting pornography and violence relayed through television, films, 'porn' magazines, and novels, it is little short of amazing that there are any good young people around at all – and it is interesting and significant that there are still so many.

In his book, *The Case Against Pornography*,† a collection of essays, David Holbrook, who edited the book, cites Rollo May, the American psychotherapist, in his famous work, *Love and Will*: '. . . many therapists today rarely see patients

* 1965.   † 1972. Tom Stacey Ltd.

who exhibit repression of sex in the manner of Freud's pre-World War I hysterical patients. In fact, we find in the people who come for help just the opposite: a great deal of talk about sex, a great deal of sexual activity. . . . But what our patients do complain of is lack of feeling and passion. . . . So much sex and so little meaning or even fun in it!'

Young people do still fall romantically in love with each other, and feel tenderness for each other in their sexual relations, I suppose; certainly one hopes so, but they cannot be oblivious of current trends and ideas, and something of it is bound to rub off on them – pornography, as D. H. Lawrence pointed out as long ago as 1929, 'does dirt on sex'. From being the 'dirty little secret' it was before World War I it has become a public obsession and degraded by pornography in all directions – very often in the name of 'culture'. It has tainted our culture; can even in a sense be said to have *become* our culture, and the intelligentsia are for the most part afraid to speak out against it for fear of being considered puritanical and reactionary . . . which in our self-consciously trendy modern world is apparently the fate worse than death.

In a letter to *The Times* (4 January 1974) on public morality David Holbook asked 'what effect does it have on young people, that adults wish to watch others do depraved things – more bizarre than anything ever done in any brothel in any historical period in the past? Whilst the critics declare that such obscenities are "not obscene". . . .' Not merely do they declare them not obscene but praise them in the most high-falutin' cultural terms. Some months ago a distinguished dramatic critic – in a distinguished Sunday newspaper – reviewed a German play which opens with a scene in which a man sits on the W.C. masturbating; no one in the audience, apparently, regarded this as anything but deeply moving, and the distinguished critic considers that this is the finest play that has come out of Germany this century. I wrote a postcard of protest to the newspaper, asking *how, why,* but it was not published, though I was promised that it would be passed on. Perhaps it was; I, anyhow, did not hear from the gentleman in response to my

G

utterly bewildered questions. Masturbation was incidentally only the opening gambit; the play went on, by all accounts, to depict on-stage defecation and fornication. I was horrified by the account, as were other liberal-minded people, who, like myself, were completely baffled that this sort of thing could be passed off as dramatic art.

But not long afterwards I read in *The Times* a review of a novel which described a sex scene so depraved as to be almost past belief. To record it turns me sideways with distaste, but unless I do readers may wonder whether or not I am being over-squeamish in the matter; and if *The Times* can record it I suppose I can. Briefly, then, the hero, whose tastes are homo- rather than heterosexual decided, after months, to 'pleasure' his wife, who has an intense desire for a child. But in order to sustain his erection to that end he fingers the backside of his boy-friend, who crouches beside the bed, during this sexual congress. I do but report. (Some, no doubt, will recognize the novel.) If this is not unutterably depraved, then the word 'depravity' has no meaning – surely? But for *The Times* reviewer it was 'a magical moment of comedy', provoking 'guffaws of pleasure and chuckles of contented amusement'. He added that the 'crudeness' was 'kept in check by wit of the most refined nature'; he found the novel 'a treasure house of riches and delicacies', and behind it an intelligence 'that sees a great echoing well of comedy at the core of every human vice and virtue'. That, I submit, is a very considerable statement, and the more it is reflected upon the less valid does it become. I further submit that it is, in fact, nonsense. And that such depravity can receive high literary praise, that such a book can be published by a reputable publisher and not even considered pornographic by them or the literary intelligentsia, is a measure of our cultural and moral decadence. To this pass are we come; to this depth of grossness are we sunk.

To be amused by depravity, in novels, films, stage and television plays, is a symptom of the hardening of the moral arteries. The contemporary cynical retort to that is, I am sure, 'So what?' But *what* is at stake is nothing less than what remains of our civilization itself. 'So what?' is the retort of a sick society.

There are those who maintain that violence, as depicted on television and in the cinema, and portrayed in fiction, is far more pernicious, or potentially so, than pornography, particularly in its impact on the young. I do not think we can choose between evils, and pornography and violence are anyhow in a sense inseparable and the one breeds the other. For the young violence is the more immediate danger; films depicting violence – particularly when it is associated with sex – can hardly fail to make a profound impression on adolescents, hardening them into an acceptance of savagery as a way of life, blunting their sensibilities. Social workers do, in fact, attribute much of juvenile delinquency to the influence of television violence. There will always be a case for the censorship of films, in the cinema and on television, since they command such vast audiences, and there is a moral responsibility on the part of the adult world to protect the young, who, being impressionable, are highly vulnerable to corruption. (The protective clause about 'not under sixteen' and 'accompanied by an adult', in respect of films shown in cinemas is inoperable, and anyhow ineffective, and with television, of course, there is not even this flimsy protection.)

Ideally, film and stage producers, and publishers, would agree, under moral persuasion – from some kind of 'watch committee', perhaps – not to produce films, plays, revues, novels, which offend common decency and are 'liable to corrupt', but such is the state of the nation that there is money – *big* money – in the cultural cultivation of pornography and violence. And as David Holbrook himself asks, 'How do we apply sanctions?' We are thrown back, it would seem, upon the forlorn hope of a spiritual renaissance.

The communist countries appear not to have these problems of pornography and violence, and that all this moral and cultural corruption we in the West are experiencing, three-quarters of the way through the twentieth century, is the decline and fall of the capitalist society is surely self-evident. It is not a question of politics, of being for or against communism, but simply of economics. Under the capitalist system the vicious circle of wages pursuing prices and prices determined by wages, is inescapable. The demand

of any government for a wage freeze, when ultimately faced
by inflation, is useless unless it can impose a prices freeze,
which in a system based on profits it cannot – and the
fantastic difference between the salaries of members of the
government and the wages of even the highest paid manual
workers – the people who actually *produce* – does not help.
But so long as we have this system of production for profit
we shall have this anomaly.

Am I, then, preaching communism? With a small c I am.
I see no alternative. Production has either to be for use, for the
benefit of society as a whole, or it has to be for profit – that is
to say for the benefit of a minority of shareholders. Workers
cannot reasonably be expected to work with loyalty and
enthusiasm for the production of private profit, and profit-
sharing schemes are, they know, nothing of the kind, but
merely the crumbs from the shareholders' table. Ideally,
industry and commerce would be run by workers' syndicates,
free of any central government – anarcho-syndicalism – but
I write as a Tolstoyan anarchist, averse to the State in any
form, Capitalist, Communist, Fascist. I think that Man,
anyhow in the Western world, moves further and further
away from this ideal, in a welter of materialism and self-
seeking; with the collapse of the capitalist system he may be
overtaken by a Western variation of communism, but that is
as far as he will go – and communism is based on centralized
government – that is to say the State. It could be, nevertheless, a big march forward from the capitalist State. It would
be a more egalitarian society. The price to be paid in loss
of freedom, political and social, is debatable. Communism
is capable of many forms. I was not impressed by what I saw
of it in Russia in 1934 and 1935, for the U.S.S.R. is certainly
not a classless society, and by all that I read and hear of it is
still not today. What I read and hear of Communist China
seems to me good, but I have not seen for myself, and, also,
what prevailed before the revolution was such that almost
anything different was bound to be better. That the whole
of the Far East, and South East Asia, will eventually go
communist I do not doubt; it will do so because of the
extremes of poverty that prevail for the multitudinous
masses and for which communism offers a solution, which

nothing else does. The price to be paid will be freedom, but what is such an abstract as freedom compared with enough to eat and a secure roof over your head? In the affluent, over-fed West, those who have not seen it can have no conception of what poverty means in the Third World, where people, men, women and children, do actually die of starvation. In Bombay and Calcutta you can see people who are virtually walking skeletons. I know, because I have seen.

I was interested in an item in the *Christian Aid Newsletter* (12 May 1975): 'Parallel with the churches' campaign in Britain ("Live simply that others may simply live") Norway is running a campaign entitled "The future in our hands", described as a popular movement for a new lifestyle and a just sharing of the world's resources. The Popular Action's permanent information and contact centre is telling people of the need for new development, through radio and T.V., press, by lectures and through the movement's own maga-zine. Among thousands of members are Thor Heyerdahl, Georg Borgstrom and the leader, Erik Dammaan.'

Man's relentless destruction of his environment through greed, pollution and irresponsibility, must be of concern to all serious-minded people. In *Industry and Environment*, published by the European Commission, in the issue of 11 February 1975, there was this: 'Cherishing the environ-ment, calling a halt to this dangerous exploitation of resources, wastage, pollution and gadgetry presupposes that man is going to change his attitude to nature, become aware, as his ancestors instinctively were, of his close dependence on all forms of life and the earth's limited resources. This calls for a new social anthropology based on an ecological ethic; man would be restored to his place in the universe, no longer dominated by terrible forces as he was in primitive society, but no longer destroying and exploiting as he does today under the influence of nineteenth-century ideologies. This implies a complete reversal of priorities and economic behaviour.'

It does, indeed, but in the affluent West few care. Farm-lands, orchards, woodlands, the countryside, are swallowed up for the creation of more and more motor-roads to accommodate more and more cars. England is becoming more and more like California, where you cannot go for a walk, where you are not *supposed* to be a pedestrian, but only a creature in a tin box on wheels. (In Los Angeles you *cannot* be a pedestrian because, in a city made for cars, there simply is nowhere to 'pedest'.)

Despite the violence and the pornography, the materialism and the greed, I do not see the contemporary scene as entirely deplorable; on the contrary there is much to admire. In the late twentieth century Western society is splendidly free – not in terms of that sexual licence we call 'permissiveness', and which is in fact decadence, but in the real terms of human beings who feel themselves free to stand up for what they believe to be their rights, and who do so undeterred by any fear of the consequences imposed by the establishment. Sixty years ago people were deterred from asserting themselves from a dread of being 'summonsed' – to appear before a court – and the fear of imprisonment. Today there is no such fear; there is no longer a stigma attached to imprisonment; it can even be a form of accolade. This attitude means that human beings can no longer be pushed around; the under-privileged no longer go abjectly for what used to be called 'relief'; they take over unoccupied premises, if need be, and demand that something be done about them. A spirit of militancy moves amongst the masses when confronted with social injustice, and this I find entirely admirable.

I have never been what used to be called a 'feminist' because, as a revolutionary socialist, I have always seen the struggle of women for social equality as part of the general egalitarian struggle. Given a true socialist society the rights of women would be a natural part of the Rights of Man. But since we are nowhere near that ideal society the rights of women, in the face of social and economic inequalities, demand attention, and, naturally, have my support. 'Women's Lib' has always seemed to me a somewhat overwrought movement, but when it comes to the-rate-for-the-job I am with them. And I could scarce forbear to cheer when I read and heard that some ten thousand women, from all over the country, rallied in London in the summer of 1975 to demonstrate against the Abortion Amendment Bill which would make abortion illegal for all but the strictest medical cases – which has anyhow long been the position. The demonstrators called for abortion 'on demand' – the right of women to control their own destinies. The demonstration was by all accounts the biggest in London since the C.N.D. protests of the 'fifties and the Vietnam campaign in the sixties. It is interesting that the Festival of Light and the Order of Christian Unity which organized a counter demonstration – with the slogan 'let babies live' – rallied less than three hundred people.

Amid all the decadence it is heartening, as I see it, that people will still demonstrate in their thousands in the cause of freedom, social and political. It is heartening, too, that with all that can be said against young people for their sexual excesses and drug addition neverthless very many young people have an intense social consciousness, which sends them on sponsored walks for good causes, and overseas on arduous and sometimes dangerous relief work. And that there are people with the courage and integrity to opt out of urban life and take up smallholdings, or form farming communities and one way or another make their own practical contribution to an alternative society . . . the 'Survivalists' of whom Patrick Rivers writes in his book*. He himself travelled thousands of miles in the U.S.A. to meet a cross-section of them before putting his own ideas into practice here – ideas of a life more in accord with Nature than that of 'technology, misapplied in the pursuit of greed'. It is not necessary, as he says, to grow a beard and eat brown rice, and certainly undesirable that inexperienced people 'should rush out to the land and try to husband it'; what is important is to realize the nature of our society and the necessity for change. 'If change does spread,' Patrick Rivers writes, 'the days of the consumer society with its dependency on monopoly capitalism, jobs, and centralized authority are numbered', adding that 'Transition to a society based on new values will not be accomplished without pain and discomfort – though hopefully with far less violence than the maintenance of the present one insidiously inflicts each and every day.'

* The Survivalists, 1975.

Since writing the foregoing, Dr Mervyn Stockwood, Bishop of Southwark, has been in hot water and accused of being a Communist with a capital C because he criticized the Archbishop of Canterbury's appeal to the nation to turn its back on materialism and seek a new moral purpose. Dr Coggan's appeal was unfortunately flat and uninspiring – what unbelievers could only regard, if they regarded it at all, as the usual ecclesiastical waffle. Whereas Dr Stockwood pointed out that 'an economic system which is based on selfishness and greed, and which leads to class divisions, injustice, and unemployment, is bound to produce social chaos'. He declared that 'a man's character, be it good or bad, is partly if not largely determined by his environment, by the social and economic circumstances in which he is placed'. Not many intelligent people would quarrel with that, but the bishop – recklessly – went on: 'Moreover, those of us who have visited socialist countries in Europe know that if a communist government were to be established in Britain the West End [of London] would be cleared up overnight, and the ugly features of our permissive society would be changed within a matter of days. And heaven help the porn merchants and all engaged in the making of fortunes through the commercial exploitation of sex.'

It is just a pity that Dr Stockwood said all this in the columns of the communist newspaper, the *Morning Star*. If he had only said it in a letter to *The Times*, although he might not have escaped their scathing editorial, 'Sad, Silly and Wrong',* his views might nevertheless have met with more temperate criticism instead of a general jumping to the conclusion that he is an uncritical admirer of communist regimes. Canon John Collins, to his credit, was quick to defend him from the pulpit in St Paul's, declaring that the bishop was not a communist but a Christian socialist.

To find virtue in certain aspects of communist regimes does not make one a communist. I, for one, find much to admire, from all I hear and read, in the People's Republic of China, but I am not a communist, since, as an anarchist, I am fundamentally opposed to that centralization of government, the *State*, which is the essence of Marxist communism.

* *The Times*, 1 November 1975.

Because Dr Stockwood has found things to admire in the socialist countries he has visited by no means makes him a communist – he has, in fact, as he reminds his critics in a letter to *The Times* (4 November 1975), been on the Soviet black list for several years because of his denunciation – in a speech to the House of Lords (reported in *Hansard*) – of the Russian invasion of Czechoslovakia. He has also, he says in his letter, many times 'spoken against Soviet tyranny, the police state and the suppression of personal freedom'.

But with all that is objectionable in the various communist regimes the fact does remain that the communist countries are not polluted by pornography and plagued by violence as are the capitalist countries of the West. Dr Stockwood wants us to 'learn from other systems', and to 'press ahead with the reformation of our own society'. He mentions Dubcek's 'socialism with a human face' and wants us to 'alter the social and economic conditions which make for irresponsibility and ugly behaviour'. That 'patterns of society and of morality are largely determined by economic conditions', as the bishop maintains, seems to me indisputable. In our profit-motivated society there is little room for community sense; the drive is for self, for ever-increasing affluence – that bloated word – for material possessions; things. In such a society freedom degenerates into licence, and pornography and violence are the natural outcome; lacking ideals, moral standards, principles, each for himself, 'anything goes', with its Hedonist philosophy of what-does-it-matter, who cares, what-harm-does-it-do. But the harm that it does is self-evident in the increasing violence, the increasing disregard for the rule of law, and the spiritual and cultural decline into decadence.

Why when even in this 'permissive' society there is an attempt to save people from physical self-destruction by clamping down on the purveyors of hard drugs, should it be considered 'repressive' and 'anti-democratic' similarly to clamp down on the purveyors of hard porn, in an attempt to save people from spiritual self-destruction, I do not understand. That the existing order is, as Dr Stockwood says, 'at last crumbling into ruins', I do not doubt, but the new and better order which must succeed it is hardly yet dormant in the West; meanwhile, in our war against pollution – of the air, our rivers, the sea, the land – we could well add war on the moral and cultural pollution of pornography. It would speed the day.

19

The lights in the valley

After the 'required reading' for the reflections on pornography it was a relief to get back to the serenities of *The Private Papers of Henry Ryecroft*, which was life in south Devon as Gissing never really knew it during his two years in Exeter. The book, which purports to be the journal of a middle-aged literary recluse, a retired writer, was written in six weeks in France shortly before Gissing died there. Henry Ryecroft is supposed to be an 'elderly' man of fifty-three; Gissing was ten years younger when he wrote it. It is his fantasy of retirement, of being freed from the struggle to make a living as a writer and having nothing to do but 'read all day long', except for walks in the Devon lanes and along the seashore – a *modus vivendi* of which, with his restless temperament, he must surely very soon have tired, since even the city of Exeter drove him back to London after two years.

But the little Ryecroft book makes pleasant reading, and leaving all the 'nature notes' out of it I found, re-reading it after a lifetime, much that spoke to my condition. Such, for example, as Ryecroft's comment on the visit of a successful writer who stayed with him for two days, and he wished he could have stayed a third, with the parenthesis that 'beyond the third day I am not sure that any man would be wholly welcome. My strength will bear but a certain amount of conversation, even the pleasantest, and before long I desire solitude, which is rest.' One does not really believe in this retired writer, Ryecroft, and his contentment in his solitary life of reading and communing with Nature; it is all too obviously the fantasy of a harassed professional writer struggling in London – the source of his material – to make ends meet, but when he is not sentimentalizing about the hedgerows and bird-song, and the pleasures of solitude in the rural setting, some of the observations on life outside all this are of interest, as when his thoughts turn to London and concerts and art exhibitions, which, in the country, he reflects wistfully, he can only enjoy in memory. He admits that he always reads the newspaper articles on exhibitions, and tries to persuade himself that this is much better after all than really going to London and seeing the pictures themselves, when he would 'try to see too many at once, and fall back into my old mood of grumbling at the conditions of modern life'. This, of course, is not really Ryecroft's content in rural retreat but Gissing straining after London from Exeter. This Ryecroft, too, for all his exultings in the joys of solitude in the country, has a man to work for him in his garden, and an 'excellent woman, an unusually good servant', to minister to him as housekeeper, bringing him his tea-tray when he comes in pleasantly fatigued by his afternoon walk in some favourite lane.

It is all very old-world and cosy and charming, but somehow in the late 'seventies, when we most of us prepare our own tea-trays and grub in our own gardens, it doesn't quite do. It, none of it, truth to tell, quite does any more, this serene withdrawal from the grunt and sweat of everyday life, coupled with a lofty, condescending pity for those – the great mass of people – unable to achieve such escape. Even in 1903 there were pressing social problems, and no man was an island then any more than now. Those of us who retire to the country now do not escape into idyllic communings with Nature, and have no wish to; we remain involved with the *Sturm und Drang* of our world even at a degree or two removed from it.

Gissing, who had in him the makings of a classical scholar but was denied the opportunity to develop this potentiality, makes Ryecroft record that 'scholarship in the high sense' was denied him, but depicts him 'gloating over Pausanias' and promising himself to read every word of him. He has Ryecroft reading Sainte-Beuve's *Port-Royal*, a massive work which he has hitherto had no time to read; he has him re-reading Shakespeare's *Tempest*, *Tristram Shandy*, which he had not opened for twenty years, the correspondence between Goethe and Schiller, Tennyson's poetry, Homer's *Odyssey*, Walton's *Life of Hooker*. With excitement he reads established classics like Sainte-Beuve's for the first time, but also renews acquaintance with old favourites, and vows that once more before he dies he will read *Don Quixote*. His reading is always on the classical level.

My own reading, in my first eighteen months or so here, has been – except for re-reading Conrad, Tomlinson, and Cunninghame Graham, and the letters of Keats, and of Gissing, which I read for this book – of contemporary writers. From my own knowledge of India in 1949 I tremendously enjoyed James Cameron's 'seventies account of it, *An Indian Summer*, published in 1974, but it is such first-rate reportage that I am sure that anyone who did not know India at first-hand, but who enjoyed a vivid, lively travel book, would similarly find it fascinating. I admired James Cameron as a fine journalist in the old *News Chronicle* days, and in this book his trained journalist's eye misses nothing, but the book is very much more than keen journalistic observation; it is compact of a deep feeling for the tragic, teeming, hopeless, exciting sub-continent. He records that for twenty-five years he has been asking himself why he must always return 'to this tormented, confused, corrupt, futile and exasperating place', as though he loved it and needed it, as though he 'had to be forever reminded of its hopelessness and the splendour of its sorrow'. Finally he married an Indian, so, as he puts it, is now 'bodily and mentally' part of the scene. But apart from its vivid evocation of the Indian scene the book 'spoke to my condition' – as the Quakers say – in personal touches. When, for example, Cameron writes that he supposes that he is 'at heart, in everything but politics, a rooted conservative' – apropos of retaining the past – he speaks for me too.

An Indian Summer was undoubtedly my book-of-the-year for 1975, but I did also very much enjoy Tony Parker's account of life in lighthouses of all kinds, and the men who man them, and their wives, *Lighthouse*, published that year. I found it both absorbing and informative.

I read Gordon Rattray Taylor's *How to avoid the future*, a kind of Doomsday handbook, for review in *The Freethinker*, and was interested and mainly in sympathy, though he doesn't really produce a blue-print for avoiding the impending doom. Which Patrick Rivers, in his new book, *The Survivalists*, with his alternative society, does. It's return-to-the-land, of course, but he himself has done it – as have others, of whom he writes.

For pleasure I read Laurie Lee's charming collection of pieces, autobiographical, travel, reflective, *I can't stay long* (so poetic a book surely deserved a more poetic title). I enjoyed, especially, his impressions of places I know – Beirut, Connemara, some Italian towns – and the frequent poetry of his prose. But whilst I would agree that Amsterdam, with its tree-lined canals, little bridges, and graceful old houses, is an attractive city – as I remember it from many years ago – I was startled, and shocked, that Laurie Lee found it 'as beautiful as Venice'. Venice is, surely, *incomparably*, the most beautiful city in the world.

I found in re-reading Conrad that whereas I could re-read the old favourites – *Heart of Darkness, Victory, Lord Jim* – and some of the short stories – notably *Amy Foster* – for the first time, with interest and pleasure, I could not read the major works, now, for the first time; I failed to read *Chance*, and *The Secret Agent, Nostronomo*, and I do not think I shall ever succeed in doing so – *The Secret Agent* seemed to me, in fact, a quite horrible story, with the wife cutting her husband's throat and then committing suicide, in her flight from the police, by going overboard a cross-Channel steamer; not that I believed in her as either homicide or suicide. *Chance* defeated me by the intervention of 'Marlow' as narrator, a devious device which presents so many of Conrad's stories at second-hand, detracting from their emotional impact, and their credibility.

I have the continual longing to read something new, and to that end I read all the book reviews in *The Times* and the *Sunday Times*, but seldom find anything which impels me to write to my bookseller or to the librarian friend who so accommodatingly sends me anything in which I express interest. The novels seem to be mostly concerned with variations on the sex theme – Mick is unfaithful to Sue, whose reactions are complicated by her relations with Sandra, or Mick's with Martin; the good old-fashioned triangle has become a quadrangle, which makes a change, I suppose, but in turn becomes a bore. One is not moved by compassion for or interest in these puppets who jerk about in sexual antics across the contemporary scene. Far away and long ago – and never no more, it would seem – the agonies and ecstasies of Galsworthy's Forsytes, and the unfamiliar but desperately real men and women of Steinbeck's novels. Novelists don't come that size any more, it seems, which is strange since life itself looms larger and more menacingly.

As a footnote to my reflections on the contemporary sex-obsession: I went the other day into the village stores-that-sells-everything to buy a dishcloth. Whilst waiting to be served I noticed a pile of what appeared to be mini panties, and then read the card which advertised them: TO CLEAR. KNICKER DISH-CLOTHS. 20p. I was still regarding them with astonishment and distaste when the shop-keeper, having disposed of his previous customer, came over to attend me. 'Good value,' he said. 'Two for only two pence more than the price of one! You undo the bows and pull out the stitches down the middle, and you've got two cloths!'

He had nothing else, so whilst protesting at the fatuousness of the idea I bought the ridiculous little 'knickers' and duly untied the absurd nylon bows at the waist and each leg, and pulled out the stitches, and then had two very small dish-cloths. With each pair of 'knickers' was a card with a verse urging that one need not be afraid to lose one's breeches, just untie the bows and pull out the stitches. . . . But why? Why must even the harmless necessary dish-cloth be presented sexily? The question is rhetorical. In the scene in which anything goes even a dish-cloth has to be sexy – and there is still scope of human ingenuity in the creation of the sexy duster and floor-cloth. As for teacloths, there is room there for all-you-ever-wanted-to-know-about-sex – at a single swipe, as it were. But it takes a Devon village to produce knicker dish-cloths. . . .

The ceremony of innocence drowned in the washing-up water!

(Oh, that 'ceremony of innocence'. What did Yeats mean by it anyway?)

Soon after I came to live here, a London acquaintance, apprised of my change of address, wrote that he hated to think of me 'cruising along' in retirement in a Devon backwater, after my interesting and adventurous life. I inquired, on a postcard, what he expected me to be doing in my seventies – living-it-up in London? Having affaires? Commuting between London and New York? Septuagenarians do, to be sure, and *chacun à son goût*, but I am of those who maintain with Browning that 'there's a decency required', and for me that decency is violated by the spectacle of elderly people trying to imitate youth, desperately trying to deceive themselves and others that the years don't count, and making themselves ridiculous in the process. There is no subsitute for youth, and the old know it; we know it, if we are honest, already in middle-age. Youth is golden and beautiful, exciting and wonderful – anyhow, it should be; if it's not, then it's a sad waste; middle-age is the time of mental and emotional maturity; it is a good time, when one is still near enough to youth to be physically attractive, still possessed of mental and physical vigour, yet sufficiently removed from youth to be free of its brashness. I have long contended that thirty-five is the ideal age for both men and women – you then still have your looks, plus as much sense as you are ever going to possess; forty-five is still all right, though the glow of youth has definitely gone by then; by the fifties you acknowledge that youth is well and truly over, the sun definitely going down behind the hill, and you become resigned to going-on-for-sixty. By the time you get there you face the fact, if you are sensible, that you are old. Any slight resistance to the idea is disposed of, finally, if you achieve the three-score-and-ten.

From then on, it seems to me, the important thing is to keep going, in reasonable health, and with such dignity as one can sustain, with no aspirations to be thought 'wonderful' for one's age – which is a form of patronage, and hardly

to be borne by any self-respecting person – but just to acknowledge that this is it, that now one is old, and that one is
lucky to be out and about, fairly fit, mentally and physically,
and with luck perhaps not too hideous. Fortunate, too, is to
have, still, some old friends left over from youth, now old
like oneself, but whom it is still a pleasure to meet from time
to time. I count myself fortunate in having a few such
friends. We meet as equals, with shared memories, and an
equal decline of energy. Because you yourself rest in the
afternoons it is a kind of comfort to learn that dear old X and
Y both do, though Y is, perhaps, a little your junior. . . . It
means that you yourself are not doing too badly. . . .

It is better, when you are old, to stay within your own age
group for friends, for outside it they don't understand; they
will one day, if they live long enough, but by then you will
have gone; at present they don't understand why, for
example, you don't go down to the beach in the afternoons
in this lovely weather; they don't understand – how should
they? – that such energy as you are able to muster in the
mornings is spent by noon; they don't understand about the
afternoon drag; or the upsurge of renewed energy with the
first drink in the evening; and it's not worth trying to explain
it to them; they have to find it out for themselves – eventually. So you smile and acquiesce, saying yes, you must do
this and that, just to keep them happy – and also to stop
them nagging you further – but you know you won't, and
that, too, is a comfort.

For most people, I suppose, old age is the day of small
things; the day of great joys, big excitements, is over – along
with the torments and frustrations; there are no intense
pleasures, but there are small satisfactions – such as demon-
strating to yourself that you are still capable of a couple of
hours' work in the garden at a stretch, of producing a good
meal for several people, of feeling sufficiently strongly about
something to write a letter to *The Times* . . . if it comes to that,
of having enough left to say at the end of the day to write a
book. There are also the small pleasures – of sight and
sound and smell; it is still a fine thing to see the long white
line of breakers curling and crumbling the sea on a windy
day, and to see the sun go down in splendour behind the

hills on a hot one; the first hearing of the cuckoo in spring –
always curiously far away – is still somehow moving, and the
full orchestration of a thunderstorm at night still exciting.
And there are always the good smells – the strong, sharp
smell of freshly ground coffee, upon which one has always to
exclaim, as though smelling it for the first time, the pungent
seaweed smell along a shore when the tide is out, the sudden
soft sweetness of lilac in May, and the strong honey sweetness of genista in June; the warm smell of gorse when the
sun is on it, the cool smell of lavender in the evening; the
smell of strawberries – better than their taste – the smell of
mint, the smell of a clean sheet that has been dried out-of-
doors . . . there is no end to the list of good smells, and I have
never been so intensely aware of them as since I came to
live in Devon, where the smell of the sea is part of the air
you breathe, and the quietness of the village is such that even
in the holiday season, when it is full of holidaymakers, you
can hear footsteps and voices, as in Venice.

I was warned before I came here that I might not like it
as much in the summer when the visitors abounded and the
shops would be full, and the pavements – as well as the
beaches – crowded. I find, however, that I not only do not
mind the summer people but quite like to see them around;
for one thing they represent an influx of youth into a normally
elderly population, and also with their bizarre clothing they
introduce colour into the normally somewhat grey scene.
True they impede progress along the pavements, because
they stroll and are always in twos and threes, spreading out –
and frequently wheel small children in push-chairs, or have
gaggles of children attached to them; also they have a habit
of pausing to gaze in a shop window, making it necessary to
step off the pavement in order to circumnavigate them, but
undeniably they bring life to the place, and the bare brown
bodies, and the sun-suits and fancy pants, make a change
from the soberly dressed Senior Citizens, many walking with
the aid of sticks, who are all too familiar out-of-season.
During the season there are long queues at the 'bus stops, and
there is a sense in which it is not all these strangers, with their
bare brown arms and T-shirts and kids, who are the in-
truders, but you and other locals who have somehow

squeezed in with shopping-bags like gate-crashers – unsuitably dressed at that – at a party. The visitors complain a little – in the accents of London, the Midlands, and the North – about the long waits in the 'bus queues, not realizing that the half-hourly service is a special summer concession, but with the kids jigging about around them they are nevertheless good-naturedly resigned to waiting – the sea will be no bluer or warmer at Torquay – or Dawlish – and the pavements even more crowded, but on every holiday there are certain musts, and its anyhow something to do to board a 'bus for somewhere else.

They are not all, of course, seized by this restlessness; the majority seem content to saunter along the promenade, or sit on it, on benches or in deck-chairs, and gaze at the sea and the passers-by, or to sit or lie on the beaches, in various degrees of nudity, the sunbathers apparently oblivious to everything but the sun on their exposed bodies, the others, who merely sit, watching the beach scene, the shimmering sea, the scurrying of motor launches on trips to this or that cove, Brixham, or Kent's Cavern. Some write postcards, others read newspapers; some just sit – some, regrettably, with transistors beside them, among the pebbles or on the sand. Time was when, if you wanted distraction on the beach, there were Punch and Judy shows, or you paddled and poked about in rock pools, or patronized the man who came round with ice-cream wafers and cornets; but mostly, between going in and out of the sea, you just sat idly and contentedly watching the scene. There wasn't the contemporary mania for grilling in the sun, in an attempt to turn white bodies brown – a process of very dubious value from the point of view of health, and one which can even be damaging. This summer-time passion for becoming brown-skinned on the part of white people riddled with colour prejudice is very curious – and interesting. They evidently believe that 'brown is beautiful' – when it is a matter of sun-tan. For people born that colour a different standard applies, and it by no means follows that the brown-is-beautiful brigade of the summer beaches would be happy if their sons and daughters wanted to marry people who were born that colour. Many years ago, on a P & O liner to Bombay, I observed that the white sun-worshippers, spread out on deck all day turning their white skins brown, did not, commonly, mix with the Indian passengers who were just naturally that colour.

The summer visitors, like tourists everywhere, leave litter in their wake, of course, a trail of ice-cream cartons and wrappings, cigarette packets, orange and banana peel, Coca-Cola and beer tins, and paper galore. 'Of course' because human beings are like that, unfortunately, and only training the young not to be litter-louts is going to cure it. We are still, mercifully, some way behind the Japanese in this respect. In Japan, if you go to a public park for a cherry-blossom 'viewing' you must wade, literally, ankle-deep in litter. Old women go round with huge sacks, forking it up, but since people continue to pour into the parks the tide of pollution never ebbs. People and pollution, in one form or another, are inseparable, it seems.

If you live in, or near, a holiday area, you must expect the tourist tide to start flowing in, strongly, early in June, to reach the flood in August, and not ebb until the end of September. By October, as in the early spring, the only visitors are elderly people there on reduced rates, and they are fairly thin on the ground, sedate, quiet people who leave no litter trail. There is room on the pavements again, no queues in the shops, and the traffic once again so light you can walk in the middle of the road if you've a mind to. The density of the car traffic is one of the worst aspects of the summer holiday season, and the pollution it represents extends even to Dartmoor, though the walker who leaves the roads and treks off into the hinterland soon gets away from it – if, that is to say, he keeps clear of the beauty spots, where the cars congregate and the litter, accordingly, accumulates.

This house, standing on a corner, at the crest of an uphill lane, where it does not look out over the mouth of the river Teign, across to the Haldon Heights, looks out over a shallow valley that was once an orchard but which is now filled with small houses and bungalows, though orchards still rise at the far side, above the suburbanization. The suburbanization is not total, however, for there remain some old thatched houses which have been farmhouses, or the adjuncts of farms. When I first came here I regretted the building in the valley, which, when it was all orchard, must have been so beautiful; but this was unjust on my part, since this house also was built on orchard land – which is why I have the good fortune to have old apple trees in the garden. Living here I have not merely become reconciled to the built-up valley but become fond of it. It is true it is no longer an orchard, but there are many apple trees left, and in January there is the exciting glow of mimosa, followed by the rosy drifts of cherry blossom and the purple patches of lilac. In summer it is less spectacular, but there are pink and red and yellow cascades of roses on walls and pergolas – and much activity with mowers on well-kept lawns. Then as dusk falls the lights come out in the valley – first the street lamps, and then the glow of lights in windows in which the curtains are not yet closed. There is then still a glimmer of light on the water, and the sky over Dartmoor carries the fading glow of sunset.

After dark the valley is a patchwork with the lighted squares of windows, with the unbroken darkness of the orchards and fields behind climbing up to the ridge, where a solitary street lamp glimmers palely and lonely at a crossing of high-hedged lanes. Across the estuary there is an orange glitter of the lights of Teignmouth, and in the other direction the wan green lights of the village of Bishopsteignton ascending the hillside. In between there is a darkness of fields, the Haldon Heights, surmounted by the Golf Club house, whose always burning light is a kind of beacon.

By day the view across the river is attractive, the ridge wooded on its lower slopes, and a checker-board of red and green fields reaching to the crest, with the straggle of Bishopsteignton beyond. I like to see it from my sitting-room windows; it is a good 'view', and I am fascinated by the long blue trains going down to Cornwall and up to London – they bring life to the scene, and the muted sound of them, across the water, is curiously part of the silence. I am never tired of the scene, but have no wish to penetrate it, for between the Haldon Heights and the river is the road to Newton Abbot, with a nonstop stream of cars and lorries, and the occasional red double-decker 'bus, and, with no pavement, it is not meant for pedestrians. I did once walk along it, and quoth the raven. For anyone foolhardy enough, it is a twenty minutes' nightmare walk from Shaldon Bridge to Bishopsteignton – which is nothing much when you get there, except for a Norman church, and, a little outside the village, higher up, the ruins of a high stone wall, now almost smothered in ivy and incorporated into some farm buildings, which is all that is left of Bishop Grandison's summer palace, fourteenth century. There is nothing to indicate it and it is not easy to find; it is interesting, really, only as the site of the palace.

From the top of the Haldon ridge, at its highest point, at the golf course, there is a tremendous view in all directions, with the sea on both sides and the county of Devon seeming to roll away to infinity. I was taken up there by car, and at my request, on a visit to Dartmoor, but with curiosity now satisfied I have no desire to go again; I now 'know about' the other side; it is the sunny side of the river, but over here at Shaldon we get the prolonged evening sunshine and the sunsets over Dartmoor. Over here, too, there is a feeling of life which the purely rural scene lacks – except for the trains. Here we are close to the sea, and there are boats galore – trim blue-and-white painted motor launches rocking gently at anchor, yachts with red or white sails, bulky catamarans, tubby dinghies, blue and red and green, and very often the stately passage of a cargo boat, moving slowly into the estuary from the sea to dock at Teignmouth. There is the alert, patiently waiting pilot boat, and the scurrying ferry – and always the wheeling and mewing of gulls.

I enjoy going once a week into Teignmouth, by 'bus across the long bridge, or by ferry across the Salty – that part of the estuary where sea and river meet. I enjoy the liveliness of the small town, and I enjoy seeing the open sea. You can see the sea from Shaldon, to be sure, if you walk right through the village to the end of the estuary, under the high red cliffs of the Ness, but it is not the open sea as you get it from Teignmouth; nevertheless, on a clear day, you can see the long, shadowy outline of Portland Bill, and on a rough, windy day you have the excitement of the great leap and break of the waves over the sea-wall in the Dawlish direction. Whatever the weather, when in Teignmouth I go and pay my respects to the sea from some vantage point along the promenade; and there is always someone, young or old or middle-aged, leaning on the railings doing the same thing. I once watched a young man gazing intently at the sea; he was there when I arrived and he was there when I left. I wondered what he was thinking of as he stood there, alone, gazing at the sea. Whether, like Keats, he had gazed 'too deeply' into it.

In winter the sea can be grey and grim, menacing; ugly, even; but in sunshine, whether it is rattling about with white breakers or merely glimmering placid as a lake, it is always fascinating. You stand and stare – literally spellbound. It is as though you could never look at it enough to absorb its immensity and its mystery.

The lights are going out in the valley as I write this, at midnight on a warm July night. When I finally leave this small, book-crowded study to go to my bedroom – where, also, books await me – there will still be a solitary lighted window pane down below in the darkness. Someone reading late in bed, I like to think; someone as nocturnal as I am; someone who nightly observes my lighted window as I observe his – or hers – with a sense of comfort.

I do not know the people in the valley, but I soon came to know the people round about, and all are very friendly, given to leaving gifts of home-grown produce – new potatoes, lettuces, sweet-peas – on my doorstep. In the lane the other day I met a woman whose name I do not know but with whom I chatted; she had a tomato plant in one hand and some white lavatera in the other; I admired the latter, never having seen a white one before. Like the tomato plant it was a gift. 'People are always giving you things in this little area,' she said, happily. In the lane, too, the other day, I was stopped by a woman who said that she knew who I was, and she was a friend of the Russian girl with whom I had gone to Turkestan in 1935 – they had studied art at the same school, she said, and she had read my book, *South to Samar-*

kand. Small world, once again, but one somehow never gets used to it.

When I first came here, now some two years ago, I was almost immediately aware that always in the village main street there were two-women-talking, at this corner or that, outside this shop or that, sometimes, inconveniently, in the middle of the narrow pavement. 'Shaldon is a gossipy place,' I thought, faintly disapproving. But now one of the two women impeding the progress of others on the pavement is likely to be me. And when you have circumnavigated the pair of us you are quite likely to meet me again a little farther on, gossiping with another woman, outside the library or the post-office or on a corner. Nor do I necessarily know the name of the woman with whom I stand gossiping; it is not necessary to; we know each other by sight, in our daily to-ings and fro-ings. Some of the women I do, of course, know by name, and one, at least, has become a friend. She, too, is a Londoner.

Two questions I am commonly asked by my London friends, in letters, and when they visit me, are 'But what is it like in the *winter*?' and, 'Do you ever think of Oak Cottage?' In the matter of weather winter is, of course, easier in the West Country than in London and the south-east. There is a good deal of wind and rain, but not much in the way of frost, and by the end of January the mimosa is in full flower everywhere – already, as I write this in mid-July, the flower buds are forming in readiness for that exciting New Year event.

As to Oak Cottage, I think of it sometimes, but only transiently; it belongs to the past – and I was never one to live in the past. In the present, though, I find I cannot grow such fine roses as I grew in London, and this disappoints me – for I planted a lot of the old favourites and they came to little or nothing – I nevertheless have large compensations – I have the big old mimosa tree to fascinate me with its Mediterranean beauty in January, and the gnarled old apple trees with their pink and white blossom in May – and all the time the view across the estuary and the sunsets over Dartmoor . . . and I see my daughter more days than not, instead of only a few times a year. I count my blessings, and they out-weigh the losses. Overhill, no less than Oak Cottage, is a house-of-character, and is as right for me in my old age as Oak Cottage had been in my youth. From the moment I came to the white field-gate to the drive and saw the estuary between the apple trees flanking the drive, and the white house, standing high, I 'knew', that, yes, I could live here; and when you know, instinctively, without having to decide you cannot be wrong.

This book has told the story of the retreat to the West, along with some reflections in – and on – retirement. In general the reflections would have been the same had I not left London, it is true, since basic ideas and attitudes to life do not change with change of habitat, but without the material and psychological relaxation of this retirement I might not have felt moved to set them down. Whether it has been a good thing to have done this is for the reader to decide. Your professional writer – and we are a dying breed – puts ideas on paper in the hope of interesting, and/or entertaining. My last autobiographical book, *Stories from my Life*, published in 1971, has produced a number of appreciative letters, for which I am very grateful, and this is the last story – the sunset story. Not as romantic and exciting as the high noon story, but interesting, it is humbly hoped, on its own after-glow level.

> *'Sunset and evening star,*
> *And one clear call for me !'*

We learned it at school, as a song, Nobody, I suppose, reads Tennyson nowadays – except, perhaps, some of my generation, finding that the modern poets do not speak to our condition. Thus, unlike Dylan Thomas, I would not wish to 'go gentle into that good night', nor feel any urge to obey his injunction to 'rage against the dying of the light' – which would seem unreasonable, and anyhow far too exhausting. Had Dylan Thomas lived to be old he might well have written as Tennyson did on the subject of that last good night:

> *'Twilight and evening bell,*
> *And after that the dark!'*

Fair enough. When it comes to it 'the dark is light enough.'

Index